DEATH ROLL

Fargo rolled the dice. They came up craps again. Fargo had had enough. He stared hard at the gambler who ran the game and the stick man who started to sweep up the dice.

Fargo's hand knocked the stick away. "Don't touch those dice," he warned.

The gambler's eyes flared. His right hand dropped below the rim of the crap table, but his Colt hit the wooden floor an instant after Fargo's slug went into his heart. The impact hurled the gambler into the men grouped behind him.

Fargo waited. He knew all those men had guns. He wondered how many were going to draw . . . and die . . .

① SIGNET (0451)

RIDING THE WESTERN TRAIL

☐ **THE TRAILSMAN #91: CAVE OF DEATH by Jon Sharpe.** An old friend's death has Skye Fargo tracking an ancient Spanish treasure map looking for a golden fortune that's worth its weight in blood. What the map doesn't include is an Indian tribe lusting for scalps and a bunch of white raiders kill-crazy with greed.... (160711—$2.95)

☐ **THE TRAILSMAN #92: DEATH'S CARAVAN by Jon Sharpe.** Gold and glory waited for Skye Fargo if he could make it to Denver with a wagon train of cargo. But first he had to deal with waves of Indian warriors who had turned the plains into a sea of blood. (161114—$2.95)

☐ **THE TRAILSMAN #93: THE TEXAS TRAIN by Jon Sharpe.** Skye Fargo goes full throttle to derail a plot to steamroll the Lone Star State but finds himself with an enticing ice maiden on his hands, a jealous spitfire on his back, and a Mexican army at his heels. Unless he thought fast and shot even faster, Texas would have a new master and he'd have an unmarked grave. (161548—$2.95)

☐ **THE TRAILSMAN #96: BUZZARD'S GAP by Jon Sharpe.** Skye Fargo figured he'd have to earn his pay sheparding two beautiful sisters through a Nebraska wasteland swarming with scalphunting Indians ... but it looked like nothing but gunplay ahead as he also rode into a clan of twisted killers and rapists called the Bible Boys that were on the hunt for bloody booty and perverse pleasure. (163389—$3.50)

☐ **THE TRAILSMAN #97: QUEENS HIGH BID by Jon Sharpe.** Bullets are wild when Skye Fargo tries to help three enticing beauties find an outlaw who left his brand on them and the Trailsman faces a pack of death dealers in a showdown. (163699—$3.50)

☐ **THE TRAILSMAN #98: DESERT DESPERADOS by Jon Sharpe.** Skye Fargo crosses into Mexico following a stolen statue worth its weight in blood, and stumbles across wagon trains filled with corpses and villages turned into cemeteries. The Trailsman is about to find himself riding straight into a showdown with trigger-happy *banditos* that few would survive.
(164083—$3.50)

☐ **THE TRAILSMAN #99: CAMP SAINT LUCIFER by Jon Sharpe.** Skye Fargo blazes away against an infernal killing crew as he follows a terror trail of corpses to a secret encampment where men kill like savages.
(164431—$3.50)

Buy them at your local bookstore or use this convenient coupon for ordering.
NEW AMERICAN LIBRARY
P.O. Box 999, Bergenfield, New Jersey 07621

Please send me the books I have checked above. I am enclosing $_____
(please add $1.00 to this order to cover postage and handling). Send check or money order—no cash or C.O.D.'s. Prices and numbers are subject to change without notice.

Name_____
Address_____
City_____ State_____ Zip Code_____
Allow 4-6 weeks for delivery.
This offer, prices and numbers are subject to change without notice.

CAMP ST. LUCIFER

by

Jon Sharpe

A SIGNET BOOK

NEW AMERICAN LIBRARY

A DIVISION OF PENGUIN BOOKS USA INC.

PUBLISHER'S NOTE

This is a work of fiction. Names, characters, places, and incidents either are the product of the author's imagination or are used fictitiously, and any resemblance to actual persons, living or dead, events, or locales is entirely coincidental.

NAL BOOKS ARE AVAILABLE AT QUANTITY DISCOUNTS
WHEN USED TO PROMOTE PRODUCTS OR SERVICES.
FOR INFORMATION PLEASE WRITE TO PREMIUM MARKETING DIVISION,
NEW AMERICAN LIBRARY, 1633 BROADWAY,
NEW YORK, NEW YORK 10019.

Copyright © 1990 by Jon Sharpe

All rights reserved

The first chapter of this book previously appeared in *Desert Desperados*, the ninety-eighth volume in this series.

SIGNET TRADEMARK REG. U.S. PAT. OFF. AND FOREIGN COUNTRIES
REGISTERED TRADEMARK—MARCA REGISTRADA
HECHO EN DRESDEN, TN, U.S.A.

SIGNET, SIGNET CLASSIC, MENTOR, ONYX, PLUME, MERIDIAN and NAL BOOKS are published by New American Library, a division of Penguin Books USA Inc., 1633 Broadway, New York, New York 10019

First Printing, March, 1990

1 2 3 4 5 6 7 8 9

PRINTED IN THE UNITED STATES OF AMERICA

The Trailsman

Beginnings . . . they bend the tree and they mark the man. Skye Fargo was born when he was eighteen. Terror was his midwife, vengeance his first cry. Killing spawned Skye Fargo, ruthless, cold-blooded murder. Out of the acrid smoke of gunpowder still hanging in the air, he rose, cried out a promise never forgotten.

The Trailsman they began to call him all across the West: searcher, scout, hunter, the man who could see where others only looked, his skills for hire but not his soul, the man who lived each day to the fullest, yet trailed each tomorrow. Skye Fargo, the Trailsman, the seeker who could take the wildness of a land and the wanting of a woman and make them his own.

Summer, 1860, it began and ended in Colorado, during a raging storm, on a muddy street, where the Devil's worst were gathered and sent back to Hell . . .

1

Shortly after the big man had cleared Raton Pass at midmorning, the leading edge of dark, roiling clouds had burst over the breathtaking Sangre de Cristo Mountains and passed low over the trail he rode. Behind him stretched the vast desolate New Mexico Territory, raw and untamed. Somewhere ahead of his Ovaro was Walsenburg, his immediate destination.

Within minutes a sprinkle of huge raindrops dimpled the dry, soft soil around him. He had dismounted and drawn his rain slicker out of the bedroll.

Now, hours later, though the ugly near-black overcast had not unleashed lightning or thunder, the deluge continued unceasing. The slicker offered precious little relief; he was soaked.

A cold wind-driven rain lashed the big man and the Ovaro on which he rode. The stallion's jet-black fore- and hind-quarters and white midsection glistened.

At dusk the pinto's ears perked and swiveled forward. Skye Fargo glanced up from the stream of muddy water he'd been watching course through the low spots on the winding trail. On his right were several dead, gnarled black oak trees, their big, barren branches reaching toward him, not unlike an old hag's. On more than one trunk he saw the rain, and dusk's shadows seemed to cast devil's faces staring out at him.

Moments later, the vague shape of a low structure loomed out of the densely falling rain. Normally weather-beaten-gray, the wide boards of the walls were now dark of color, almost black, dulled by the steady falling rain. The gloomy building's roof slanted back at a sharp angle. A sheet of water seemed to leap from the low side of the roof and had formed its own tributary, also rushing south.

A black rectangle high enough to accommodate a mounted rider identified itself as the front entrance.

The trail quickly widened into a street. Fargo rode down its middle and past the low structure on his right, which he now recognized as a smithy. On his left was a small building. The rain-drenched sign on its front identified it: LAND OFFICE. On his right another sign painted above the door of a somewhat larger building read PEARSON'S FIREARMS. No lamps burned inside either edifice, but ahead, light spilled through windows in buildings on both sides of the street. A long line of saddled horses stood at hitching rails in front of the two-story structure on his left. The sound of piano music filtered out. Another stream of light came from what was clearly a small café.

Adjacent to the café stood another large two-story building. A slim man stood on its sheltered long front porch, his back to the front door. Fargo angled toward the man. Coming closer, he saw tall white letters that spelled BUCKHORN HOTEL on the wall over the porch. He reined the Ovaro to a halt facing the man, who he now saw was no more than forty and had a receding hairline and a thin nose. He was intensely watching the stream of mud, as though it might change course any second, spill over the porch, and come inside the hotel.

Fargo cleared his throat loudly. The man glanced up at him. Fargo said, " 'Evening, mister. I'm looking for the public stable."

The man pointed to the far corner. "It's on Dynamite Street, down a ways, on the right, next to the wagon repair. Can't miss it. Follow your nose. The stable's stink will take you straight to it."

Fargo nodded and reined the pinto that way. The Buckhorn Hotel set on the southeast corner of the intersection. Directly across from it was a barbershop. On the northeast corner stood a huge feed store, and directly across from it, on the northwest corner, was a bank. Fargo rounded the corner occupied by the barbershop. Wall-mounted lamps burned inside.

An unusually wide wagon-repair place was behind the bank. Across the street from the wagon repair and next to a sheltered high board fence behind the barbershop was a spacious corral holding at least a dozen horses. The vague shape of the stable slowly emerged in the downpour.

Rain-blurred glimmers of lantern light reflected yellow on the wet ground in the middle of the dark front opening. The strong scent of horse manure and hay emanated from the building.

As Fargo punched through the torrential downpour, he saw a barrel-chested older man with a gray beard and bushy mustache, both stained with visible evidence the man chewed tobacco. He stood in the wide opening of the tall frame structure, the lantern at his feet. His hands were jammed so far down in his pockets that the red suspenders holding the pants up were tight as banjo strings and grooving his shoulders. He was studying the swift-running stream of muddy water churning down the street, dangerously close to his business.

He lifted his studious gaze when the Ovaro walked up and Fargo reined it to a halt. "Whut cha want?" the man asked in a gruff no-nonsense tone, quickly adding, "Drifters usually hitch their horses out front of the saloon."

"I'm no drifter, old man. Got an empty stall for the night?"

"Mebbe." He cocked his head and squinted up at Fargo's chiseled face. "Have to see money first." He spat a long brown stream toward the mud flow.

Fargo understood the concern. You could count on drifters to take advantage of good-natured people. He flipped a silver dollar to him. The old man bit it to make sure it was real, then said, "Welcome, stranger." As he pocketed the coin, a dry grin rearranged his mustache. "Mite wet, ain't it? Ride on in."

He stepped back and led the way. A half-dozen horses were tethered to rungs on the boards at the far end of the alleyway separating the stalls on either side. "Cowpoke's animals," the old man explained over his shoulder. "Some like to put their horses inside. I tether 'em for two bits overnight. That way they get to piss the other six bits off gambling." His head shook solemnly. Swinging a stall gate open, he said, "Only one left. You're lucky, friend."

Fargo dismounted and stripped the Ovaro. The old

man handed him a wad of rags. Fargo began drying off the stallion.

"Mighty fine pinto you have there," the man offered. "Wouldn't want to sell him, would you?"

"Not for sale." Fargo reached inside his saddlebags and brought out the dandy brush, which he used to remove several lumps of mud from the stallion's coat. Satisfied, he returned the dandy brush and brought out the hoof pick. He started cleaning the horse's left front hoof first.

A horse rider came through the entrance. Three others quickly followed. Fargo glanced their way. None wore slickers, but all wore gun belts. As they dismounted, the old man hurried to them.

Fargo kept cleaning the Ovaro's hooves and checking the shoes, but he was alert to the conversation at the entrance. The old man was saying quite emphatically, "Private stalls? I ain't got any left. Ain't got no place to put your animals. I'm full up for the night."

"Well, you old fool, empty four," the hard voice of the bigger man ordered. "Hitch 'em outside in the rain if you have to, but we're coming in."

"Oh, you are, huh?" The old man's tone carried a fight in it. He tested the new arrivals. "I suppose you're prepared to pay double and face the owners of the horses when they come for them in the morning and I tell what happened."

"Naw, old man," the bigger man snorted, "we ain't paying double. We ain't paying nothing. Anybody wants to make something out of it, he'll get hurt. We came to see Thurston, so get them four stalls ready."

Fargo lowered the stallion's left rear hoof to the ground. He moved through the heavy shadows next to the stalls to come up behind the husky man giving the stable-owner a hard time.

"Thurston?" the old man cried, his voice now definitely angry. "Get outta my place, you sons a bitches! I don't stable drifters. 'Specially those friendly with that bastard."

"Pete, go clean out four stalls," the bigger man growled. As the old man stood his ground, saying, "You do and—" Fargo's left forearm clamped tight around the bigger man's throat. Before the men could react and go for their guns, Fargo slapped the Colt upside the head of the man he held.

When he brought the powerful forearm away, the man's knees buckled and he sunk to kneel on them. Fargo swung the Colt to aim gut-level from one to the other of the three men while hissing, "Get him on his horse and get out of here. The old man said he doesn't want your business."

Fargo watched as they obeyed him. He ingrained the images of their faces in his mind. The one he had knocked to his knees had a cruel scar across his chin and deep sunken eyes that held hate.

The shortest man had a wide nose and dark eyes that were in constant motion.

The other two men were both about six feet tall. One was lantern-jawed, the other had a short red beard sprinkled with black hairs.

The old man was wrong. They were a notch above being common drifters. Drifting, yes, but these men would murder to get what they wanted . . . and rape, and plunder. Alone, none had the backbone to do it. But as a group, they could intimidate. All four were the kind who would kill their own mothers for a nickel. Men like these, ignorant and uncaring, were highly dangerous, especially in dark places. They bore watching.

"I'll get you for this," the hurt man snarled from in the saddle. He held a palm to the side of his face and stared coldly at Fargo as they rode out.

"I'll be around," Fargo answered.

The old man booted a horse apple through the opening. "What did you butt in for?" he complained bitterly. "I coulda took care of them rotten sons a bitches all by myself."

Fargo grinned slightly and cocked his head to one side. "Sorry. I guess I underestimated you."

The old man grumbled under his breath while he followed Fargo back to the Ovaro. Fargo nudged the horse inside the stall and said, "Give him good oats and hay, plenty of water. I'll be back at dawn."

"Even if it's still gully-washing like this?" The old man's expression conveyed more concern than did his tone of voice.

Fargo closed and secured the gate. "We're used to it," he replied dryly. "Who runs the hotel?"

"Ben Voss and his wife, Freida, they own it. You'll find the Buckhorn right across from that no-good Douglas Thurston's new Saloon and Gambling Emporium." He paused, then grunted, "Highway-Robbery Emporium if you ask me."

Fargo leaned against the gate and rested a boot on the bottom slat. "Oh? What do you mean by that? Are you saying this man, Thurston, cheats?"

The old man scratched in his beard. "Don't rightly know, mister. Let's say ain't nobody caught him at it. But there ain't a man alive who has that much good luck. Leastwise I ain't never met such a man . . . till Douglas Thurston came to Walsenburg 'bout six months ago, that is."

"What does your sheriff have to say about it?"

The old man scowled. "Hunh. Thurston had Howard an' his deputy, Earl Davidson, shot dead first thing after he came to town. Right in front of the saloon. Two cowards did it for him. Didn't see it myself. Folks who did said they was devils. One was only half a man—a dreadful sight, I'm told—an' the other had a long scar on his face." The old man drug a fingernail down the left side of his face. "The sons a bitches shot 'em in the back. We ain't got no sheriff. Everybody's afraid to wear the badge."

Fargo draped the saddlebags over his shoulder and carried the Sharps in his hand. He headed for the opening, commenting, "Maybe Thurston isn't all that lucky."

The old man hurried to catch up. He snorted, "Whaddaya mean by that?"

"Maybe the rest of you give him his good luck."

"How's that?" He tugged on Fargo's shirt sleeve to make him wait and explain before stepping out in the rain.

"While many sit to gamble, few know how. Where do I get a hot bath?"

"Fred Hushour's barbershop is next door to the saloon. Fred, he can fix you up with a bath for a nickel. Whaddaya mean, 'few know how?' "

"Just what I said." Fargo glanced at the black sky, then stepped out in the rain and mud.

Behind him the old man grumbled, "Dammit, mister, come back here and tell me what you meant by that. You . . ." His voice trailed off, absorbed by the rain.

At the Buckhorn the man on the porch smiled and shook his head when Fargo walked up and joined him.

"You Ben Voss?"

"Yes, sir."

"Got a room for the night?"

"Eight, in fact. But that will change in a few hours." Voss's eyes cut past Fargo to the saloon.

Fargo looked at the noisy establishment barely visible through the hard, steady rainfall. "How long does that racket go on?"

"Until all the suckers go home flat broke . . . or pass out."

Fargo chuckled. "That old man at the livery said much the same. Sounds like you people have a problem."

"Neil Kaspar? Well, he ought to know. Thurston's took just about all Neil owns. All he has left is the livery, and Thurston will have it by the end of the month."

"If you have one, give me an upstairs back room where I won't have to listen to that noise all night."

Ben ushered him into the small, clean lobby dominated by a splendid rack of elkhorns displayed on the wall directly above the lower steps of a narrow staircase that led to the second floor. A long mirror hung on the wall across from where a chubby, thin-lipped woman dressed in black and light-brown gingham stood behind the registration counter. Room keys hung from pegs inches from her back, an open ledger lay on the counter before her.

Ben asked her to put their guest in Number 9. She turned the ledger for Fargo to sign.

Fargo touched the brim of his soggy hat. " 'Evening, Mrs. Voss."

The schoolmarm bun coiled on her head nodded slightly.

She glanced down to watch him enter his name. "Staying long, Mr. Fargo?" Freida Voss obviously knew how to read upside down. Most teachers could. Fargo bet the serious-faced woman wielded a mean schoolroom paddle too.

"Be leaving at the crack of dawn, ma'am."

She handed him the room key. "That will be one dollar, Mr. Fargo. The stairs to the privy out back are at the end of the hall." When she next spoke, Fargo detected a look in her eyes that might have said I-don't-like-doing-it-but-we're-broke. "If you wish, I'll be more than happy to wash and iron your clothes tonight. Ben will bring them to you in the morning when you wake up. Just stomp the floor several times when you're ready. Our bedroom is below yours. Washing and ironing is twenty-five cents."

Fargo paid her. "I'll stomp on the floor when they're ready to come down to you."

"Yes, sir. Thank you for staying at the Buckhorn."

Fargo stayed in his room long enough to drop off his saddlebags and Sharps, then went next door to the café.

Two tables with red-and-white-striped tablecloths stood next to the front windows. A row of eight freestanding wooden stools were neatly spaced in a line in front of the counter dotted with salt and pepper shakers and shot glasses filled with flat toothpicks. All wall surfaces were white and looked as though they'd been freshly painted. Fargo took a stool left of center in the row.

A rotund man older than Neil Kaspar stood behind the counter, staring blankly through the rain-drenched windows. Fargo didn't know whether the fixation was on the ever-widening current of muddy water or on the saloon beyond it. Puffy coffee-hued bags bulged under the man's glazed dark eyes, deep-set in his clean-shaven beefy face.

Fargo interrupted the man's stolid gaze, saying, "Biggest steak you have. While it's cooking, keep filling a cup with hot coffee."

The man blinked, stiffened, and shouted toward an archway on his left, "Burn a steer, Millie!" He set a cup and saucer before his customer.

A young, rather attractive female poked her head and

shoulders through the opening. Dark-blue eyes batted above her nice smile as she looked at Fargo.

Without looking at her the man snapped, "Stop ogling the customers and do what I said." He turned and filled the cup with steaming brew, mumbling, "Young wives are more problems than they're worth."

Fargo swiveled around to face the saloon while he sipped from the cup. A lean man about five feet ten pushed through the saloon's swinging doors and paused under the porch's overhanging roof to raise his collar and hunch his shoulders. He dashed out into the rain, leapt the mud-swollen surge, and burst through the café door, laughing. The counter man's sullen expression took a dramatic change. Now his eyes seemed to twinkle.

Before the beaming youth—Fargo put him at twenty, no more than twenty-two—sat three stools down from him, near the open archway, Fargo noticed the youngster's big belt buckle was in the shape of Texas. He also wore a gun belt fashioned from black leather, dressed with care; water beaded on it rather than soaked in. The holster rode low on his left thigh and was held down by a black leather thong. The holster held a Smith & Wesson with ivory grips.

He said cheerily, " 'Evening, Mr. Wilson." Leaning toward the opening, he added, "You too, Mrs. Wilson."

Wilson replied, " 'Evening, Kid. Winning or losing?"

"Losing." Millie's lilting voice answered from the kitchen. "Howdy, Kid. What can I fix for my sweetie?"

"Aw, shucks, ma'am, same as always, I reckon." Fargo thought he saw a hint of a blush spread across the kid's face when she called him sweetie. When Wilson set a cup and saucer on the counter and began filling it, the young cowboy drawled, "That Thurston's the luckiest devil this side of the Pecos."

Wilson's eyes darted at the rain-slickened window as he scowled, "Yeah, well, if the son of a bitch lays his nasty eyes on Millie's ass again, I'll send him to hell and let him try double-dealing Satan." He spoke loud enough for her to hear.

She changed the subject. "Found your man yet, Kid?"

The kid swallowed some of his coffee first. "No, ma'am,

but he'll come this way sooner or later. I can't go riding all over to find the man even though Mr. Hollis said for me to. I'll just stay put a while longer and wait for him to come along."

Fargo looked at him and said, "I see you're from Texas."

"Yes, sir. Estelline."

"Ranch hand?"

"Yes, sir. I work for Mr. Richard Hollis, owner of the Bar Z Bar spread. I'm not much at dogging steers, though." Fargo saw the blush try to form again. The wrangler added, "But I make up for it in other ways."

Fargo bet he did indeed. He suspected the young man would be a deadly accurate shot, and fast as a striking rattler. His gaze lowered to the Smith & Wesson, slowly so the kid would notice.

The kid cut an easy grin that to most folks would be deceptive and put them at ease. Fargo had seen the same disarming grin in his own mirror many times. Behind the kid's grin was instant justice. Fargo wondered if the lazy upturned corners of the lips remained while the cowboy meted out his brand of swift comeuppance with the Smith & Wesson. Some law-and-order men's did, others did not.

"How's it going over at the Emporium?" Fargo nodded toward the saloon.

The kid blossomed a nice smile that presented even white teeth. "Packed house," he replied. "Only two fistfights so far this evening. The piano music is pretty good, though. No pianos in Estelline. Mostly I go there to watch and listen while I wait."

Fargo was ready to believe that the pleasant young ranch hand and himself were the only ones in town who weren't victims of the Emporium. He didn't pry for the wait-for-who. The kid had already mentioned *the* man would come along sooner or later. It sounded as though he meant a drifter or outlaw, one who would get to see the easy grin.

A thick juicy steak that overlapped the ends of the platter was placed in front of Fargo and brought an end to the budding conversation.

Before taking her hands away from the platter, Millie stared and smiled at her customer, too long for her husband. He nudged her aside and handed Fargo a carving knife, then turned his attention back to the sandy-haired cowpuncher. Millie swelled up in a huff and walked back to her kitchen.

Fargo watched her rolling rump, knowing her husband had a greater problem than he probably imagined, and the man probably imagined much.

Fargo ate, settled up with Wilson, and stood to leave. At the door he heard the sound of a shot pierce the downpour. His right hand automatically gripped the Colt's handle.

Just before it did, he heard the Smith & Wesson's hammer cock behind him.

2

The kid, Wilson, and his wife appeared at the windows on Fargo's left. With him they stared through the night rain at the saloon. Within seconds two men dragged the limp body of a man onto the porch and heaved it out into the muddy street. The man didn't get up or even move from the facedown position.

Millie whispered why. "Thurston's killed another one who called him a cheater."

Fargo opened the door and crossed over to the barbershop. A little bell above the inside of the shop's entrance tinkled when he entered. There was one barber chair with nobody in it—or the room, for that matter. The wall-mounted lamps bathed the small place of business in a cheery glow. A sheet hung over a doorway in the back wall. The room was heavy with the aroma of lilac hair tonic. A common wall separated the shop from the saloon. The piano on the saloon's side was obviously jammed against the wall, for it vibrated, especially when the deeper notes were played.

Fargo looked at his reflection in the mirror behind the barber chair, stroked his beard, and decided it was okay. A hand pulled the sheet open at one side and a worried man's face appeared.

The man was quite nervous, evidenced by a tic at the outer corner of his left eye and the fact that both his eyes darted to the pulsating wall, bounced to the front of the shop and back to Fargo.

"Yes, sir, can I help you?" the man asked in a trembly voice. "Haircut, perhaps? Need a tooth extracted?" He spoke as though he hoped not, as though he hoped Fargo would leave.

"I'm no drifter," Fargo told him. "I came for a hot bath. You Fred Hushour?"

The man stepped through the drape. He was firm of build although narrow-shouldered and no more than five and a half feet tall. He wore small eyeglasses and had a mole on his left cheek. The tic seemed to lessen as he said, "Of course. Do you want regular lye soap or the fancy kind from back East? Fancy soap is a nickel more."

"The regular soap is fine."

"Yes. Have a seat and I'll get the tub ready. Won't take but a minute or two." He backed through the sheet curtain.

Fargo sat in a straight-back at the common wall. Through the piano music he listened to a crap game in progress. A loud voice begged for a six, then yelled, "Aw, shit!" when he obviously rolled a seven. It went on and on, and he never did hear the shooters yell they made their points.

After a few moments the barber parted the sheet and announced the bath was ready. Fargo followed him out back where four large wooden tubs stood under a spacious shed open on all sides but having a watertight roof. The area was surrounded by the high board fence Fargo had seen on his way to the stable. The tubs rested on steel frames high enough to keep the flames in the fire pits below them from licking the tub's bottoms. Steps led up to the rims of the tubs. Several lit lanterns hung on wires dangling from the rafters. Fargo sat on a wood bench to pull of his boots.

Hushour asked timidly, as though someone in the saloon might hear, "Who did he shoot this time?"

Fargo shook his head. "I wouldn't know."

"That makes the third one this week. The tenth since he came to town. Walsenburg used to be a quiet, decent place to live. Not anymore, though. If it isn't Douglas Thurston disturbing the peace and tranquillity, then it's those no-good drifters that have heard he's here and flock to him."

Pulling down his Levi's, Fargo asked, "What do you mean by drifters who've heard?"

"Hellfire, mister, ever since he came, they've been

coming like bees to flowers. Most are running from the law. Thurston lets them stay in his upstairs rooms, then gives them money when they leave town. I guess it's true."

Going up the steps, Fargo asked, "What?"

"Criminals hang out with criminals. Holler if you want me to stoke the coals."

Fargo settled down into the hot water and relaxed, his broad muscular back against the curve of the tub. Listening to the rain tattoo on the roof and watching it cascade over the edges, he drifted into sleep.

The rain ceased falling abruptly. The sudden change of rhythm jolted Fargo awake. The bathwater had also changed temperature. It was now lukewarm. Fargo soaped and scrubbed his body, ducked under the floating suds to rinse off, and stepped out of the tub. As he came down the steps, Hushour opened the gate to the bath area.

"Thought I better come check on you, mister, you being out here so long."

"How long?"

"Little over an hour."

"I fell asleep."

"I know. Four men have bathed and had shaves since you came out. They told me I had a snoozer."

"The hell you say. Were they barefoot?" It wasn't like his wild-creature hearing to miss the sounds of four men, no matter how quiet. He concluded that he was more tired than he thought.

"No." Hushour chuckled. "But they were quiet. I warned them not to get loud or shoot a hole in one of my tubs." He pointed at several corks plugging holes in the side of the tub Fargo used. "Sometimes they get rowdy. Freida said your name is Skye Fargo."

Fargo buttoned his shirt and tucked in the shirttails before answering, "That's right. The old man at the livery—Neil?—said yours is Fred Hushour. Any kin to the Hushours over in Wichita?"

"Probably, but I'm from Cincinnati. Never been to Wichita. Don't suppose you need me to trim your beard and mustache. I will for a dime."

"Think I'll pass. Maybe next time I come to Walsenburg. Did anyone haul that dead man away?"

"John Schutte, he's the printer. Me and him carried the body to Doc Williamson. Doc gets all the dead folks ready to lay to rest. Reverend Orr sends 'em on their way, heaven or hell, whichever they deserve. When he isn't in the saloon, that is."

Fargo started pulling on his boots. "That saloon sounds like it's got this town tied in a knot."

"Flat broke too."

"Oh, you included?"

"Yes, sir, bad as I hate to admit it. Douglas Thurston's going to own Walsenburg and all in it within six months . . . if somebody doesn't kill him first."

"Uh, huh, that's the second threatening reference made toward him I've heard tonight. Makes me wonder why one of you hasn't already shot the man."

"Truth is, mister, all we do is talk about doing it. Can't speak for the others, but me, I'm afraid to try. Thurston's fast as lightning with a gun."

"Is he grinning when he shoots a person?"

"Oh, I should say not. No, sir, he looks mean. Blazing eyes, curled lips . . . No, he isn't grinning. Fearful sight, he is. No man can stand up to him."

"Yeah, well, how about holding that lantern out in front when you show me the way out of here?" Fargo swung his gun belt around his hips and buckled it.

Fred Hushour looked at the big Colt, as though he'd seen it for the first time. "You know how to use that gun? By that I mean, real good."

Fargo replied, "Lead the way, Fred."

Hushour went with him as far as the saloon's swinging doors. "I wouldn't go in there if I was you," the barber warned in a low tone. When Fargo grinned and winked at him, Hushour turned and headed for his shop.

Fargo surveyed the crowd before pushing through the double doors. A husky no-nonsense-looking man of about thirty roamed back and forth behind the long bar, filling shot glasses as fast as they were emptied and collecting money as he went. He wore a red apron. Considerable black curly hair showed in the long V of his partly unbuttoned white shirt.

It looked as though not one inch of the brass rail at the base of the bar didn't have a boot on it. The kid had been correct: the saloon was packed with customers, mostly cowhands.

The place was noisy as the inside of a screeching fiddle, and a blue haze of tobacco smoke filled the spacious room. Against the wall on Fargo's right stood the piano, played by a scrawny fellow wearing a top hat and a blue polka-dot shirt. A mug half-filled with beer sat on top of the piano. Next to the mug sat a leggy brunette, snapping her fingers in time with the tempo and smiling hugely.

Between the piano and bar were seven poker tables, all occupied. The upper body of a scarecrow of a man with bushy, unruly gray hair lay draped over the poker table nearest the piano. His face was pressed straight down on the tabletop. The men who sat in the other chairs held cards and didn't seem to even notice him. Standing onlookers held beer mugs or glasses of whiskey.

In an alcove at the back of the room was the crap table. It was lined with shooters surrounded by sweaters three deep. Most of the noise boiled out of the alcove. A curvy redhead had one arm curled around a cowpuncher's neck and patted his small butt with the other hand.

At the far end of the bar, left of the alcove and beyond the opening of a hallway, a narrow stairway with handrails led up through the haze to the landing on the second level. The landing extended to where the pitch of the rafters of the second story stopped it several feet short of the common wall. The opening of a hallway was on the far side of the top landing and directly above the one on the ground level. As he looked a lanky cowboy emerged from the hallway and paused on the top landing to stuff in his shirttail. His expression showed satisfaction.

By the time the satisfied cowboy got to the bottom step, a shapely redhead came through the upper hallway entrance. She wore a strapless red dress with a fringed hem that swished at her knees when she came down the stairs. She joined those crowded around the crap table.

The four men Fargo chased out of the stable sat at the

poker table nearest to the piano and at the front of the saloon. Two bottles stood in the center of the table. The men were leaned in, talking.

Fargo stepped to the bar and wedged between two of the wranglers. When the bartender came, Fargo ordered a beer. As he drank, he peered through the haze at the alcove.

The man on his left glanced up and suggested, "I wouldn't go back there if I was you. They already killed one man tonight."

Fargo ignored him and shifted his gaze to the blonde who was decorating the piano. He moved his gaze off her and to the four men still hunched over the poker table, drinking and conversing with conspiratorial expressions on their faces.

A male voice at the crap table yelled, "I'll be goddamned!" and drew Fargo's attention. "That makes the seventh time in a row them goddamn dice came up craps on me," the man complained angrily.

Fargo carried his beer with him when he went and stood to look over the shoulders of those crowded behind the man who was overseeing the game, obviously Douglas Thurston, who he had heard so much about.

Thurston sat perched on a stool with his elbows resting on the top edge of the crap table. On either side of him stood his helpers, who handled the come bets, made change, collected and paid out money. Across from him stood a tall rawboned stickman wearing a green apron with a wide pocket in front, which Fargo and all the others knew contained several pair of dice. His left hand held the slim limber shaft that was designed with its lower end curved to capture and move about the dice in play. The Trailsman noticed the young Texan in the crowd.

All Fargo could see of Thurston was his broad shoulders, neck, and head. He wore a black coat that had a shiny black collar with the top edge of a pure white silk shirt collar peaking up from inside it. The jet-black wavy hair fairly gleamed from the hair oil in it, as did the white sideburns.

Bets were placed on the pass line all around the table.

The stickman dipped a hand in his apron pocket and withdrew three pairs of dice, which he dropped on the green felt cover, then moved with the stick to the next shooter.

The shooter selected a pair. Fargo's eyes stayed on the stickman's hands. The stickman drew the discards in front of him and returned them to the pocket.

The shooter begged for a seven or eleven, rolled and caught an eight for his point. "Easy eight," one of the helpers chortled. "I'm taking come bets. All you come-bettors get down."

Hands began laying coins on the come lines. Fargo watched the stickman's right hand pass low over the pair of dice when he reached out to rearrange bets on one of the come lines.

The bettors stood and waited as the stick moved the dice back to the shooter. After shaking them vigorously for good luck, the shooter bounced the dice off one end of the table. They came up nine. All come bets were quickly moved onto the nine blocks.

Next, he tossed a four. Then snake-eyes, six, another six, then he crapped out. During the ensuing cries of disgust and slight movements of those around the table, Fargo kept his eyes on the stickman's hands. He watched the man retrieve the dice and put them in the left side of the apron pocket, slip the hand to the right side, where he removed three pairs of dice and dropped them on the table.

After watching six shooters roll points only to subsequently crap out, usually quickly, Fargo eased to one end of the table and squirmed up to it. He now viewed Thurston in profile. The man was dark-complected and handsome. He kept his head tilted down, his eyes on the stacks of money lined up next to the inside of the table where he sat, as though it wasn't necessary to look the players in the eyes, as though he was bored stiff. He wore a gun belt. A Colt just like Fargo's rested in the holster.

Along with everyone else bellied up to the table, Fargo lost two one-dollar bets, Thurston's minimum. Then the dice came to Fargo. He put a silver dollar on the pass line, glanced at Thurston's cocksure downward focus on his stacks of money, and chose a pair of dice from the curved end of the stick. Still looking at Thurston, he pitched the dice to the other end of the table. They bounced halfway back and stopped rolling in front of the stickman.

"Easy eight," a helper announced.

Come bets were made, and the stickman rearranged a few of them. The curved end of the stick bearing two dice swept across the green felt and positioned them for Fargo to grasp. He tossed the dice. "Craps," someone shouted.

The helper's hands shot out to collect the money on the pass line. Fargo knocked a hand away from his bet and said, "Whoa, mister. I think there's some cheating going on at this table."

A voice in the crowd groaned, "Mister, you ought'n've said that."

Those near Fargo parted to get out of the line of fire, to make room for the body to fall. As though by magic, a hush fell over the room.

The stickman moved to get the dice as Thurston's eyes kicked up. Grim-jawed Thurston started rising from the stool slowly.

Fargo's hand knocked the stick away from the dice. "Don't touch those dice," he warned evenly, his eyes still locked on Thurston's.

Thurston's eyes flared and he hesitated in his rise, as though he'd seen the devil himself and wasn't quite sure of what to do. The tip of his tongue parted his lips and traced across them once. Shrugging, he started to sit back down. Fargo saw Thurston's right hand drop from its grip on the rim of the crap table.

Thurston's Colt hit the grimy wooden floor an instant after Fargo shot him in the heart. The impact of the slug hurled Thurston into those grouped behind him. In his peripheral vision, Fargo saw the bartender swing a rifle up from under the bar. He brought the Colt around and fired. The bullet tore into the bartender's forehead and knocked him back into the shelves of bottles and glasses beneath the long mirror on the wall.

Fargo quick-glanced to the foursome at the distant poker table, noted that while they were looking at him, they remained seated. He shifted his gaze to stare into the stickman's nervous eyes. "Any of you who helped Thurston run this crooked game have a gun hidden on you?"

All three shook their heads. Still holding the stickman with the hard stare, Fargo asked, "What's your name, friend?"

The fellow smiled hugely. "They call me Big Daddy."

"Well, Big Daddy, I'll say one thing for you. Yours are the fastest and nimblest hands I've watched work in several years. Now, two of you losers feel all over Big Daddy's shirt and around his waist. No need to check in his apron pocket."

Two men stepped forward to do as Fargo asked. But Big Daddy apparently hadn't learned his lesson. He made a sudden movement, bringing his right arm around from behind. Fargo's shot made a neat red hole in his forehead. He dropped like a bag of rotten potatoes to the grimy floor, a small French-made hideout gun in his hand.

Fargo started reloading the Colt. As he did, he again looked at the foursome, and this time they averted their eyes.

The young Texas ranch hand looked down at Thurston's body sprawled on the floor, lying in a widening pool of blood. "Mister, are you positive he was cheating? All of us saw everything same as you. How do you know?"

Curious glances were exchanged. Boots shuffled on the floor as britches were hitched up, new stances taken. All eyes focused on Fargo as they waited to hear the answer.

Fargo holstered his Colt, glanced down at Thurston's bleeding body, then began, "The last time I saw him was on a Mississippi riverboat going from New Orleans to Natchez. Then his name was Antoine Devereaux. Fancy-dressed gambling man smoking long cheroots. He made the mistake of palming cards on me in a game of draw. I threw him overboard, into the Mississippi. Reckoned he'd drown. Guess I forgot rats can swim."

His attention shifted to the kid. "Step up to the table." The youngster did and looked down at the ruby-red dice dimpled with white dots. "What do you see?" Fargo asked.

"Well, that one on the left has the six up. There's a three on one side and the one spot on the other. The dice next to it has the one on top. On the sides are the three and six. So?"

"Now come around the table and tell what you see."

He did and said, "Six and one are up, of course. That one dice has a three and one on its sides, and the other a six and three. I don't get it."

"Pick up the die with six on top and see what's on the bottom."

Everyone strained to see when he turned it over. "I'll be a son of a gun," the kid whispered, "another six." He checked the other surfaces, cut squinted eyes at the gaping crowd, and added, "All this dice has on it are two sixes, ones, and threes." He grabbed up the other dice and inspected its surfaces. "Same numbers," he muttered.

Fargo explained, "It's impossible to see more than three surfaces on a cube without moving to one side or the other quite aways. Thurston knew this. All riverboat gamblers do. Those dice are called tops. Reach in Big Daddy's apron pocket and tell us what you find."

The crowd inched closer as the cowboy stooped to comply. "I feel three little pockets over on one side and a bigger one on the other. One of the little pockets is empty. There is a pair of dice in each of the other little ones, and let's see . . . four, five, six, eight dice in the big side."

"Haul out a pair from the big side and let's see what they look like."

The crowd leaned in. "Regular dice," the kid commented after checking all sides of both.

"Those are called straights," Fargo explained. "He put them out so you could get a point. Some people take the time to look at the dice before they roll. When they do, and everybody else is watching too, they see everything is in order on the dice and figure the game is straight, hence the name of those dice. Now get a pair from one of the small pockets."

Fargo didn't have to tell the kid what to look for, but Neil Kaspar's curious voice asked, "What's on them?"

"Nothing but the six, two, and one," the youngster answered.

"Damn," a whiskey voice cried.

"Yes," Fargo agreed. "Any way you add them up, the only odd numbers those tops will roll are the three and the seven."

Someone commented, "Three ain't a point and seven is craps."

"Right," Fargo replied. "You got these when your point was an odd number. My point was eight, an even number. The stickman switched dice on me and gave me the six, one, three. They will not come up eight or ten. You can look if you want, but the dice in the other pocket will be the six, four, one. They were used anytime the point was a four, eight, or nine."

Kaspar wanted to know more. He squeezed between two people, frowned, and asked what was on everybody's mind: "How'd the sons a bitch do it? Me and everyone else, fifty eyes was watching the bastard, them dice."

Fargo looked at him and broke a grin. "I said you people might be giving Thurston his luck. Remember me telling you 'few know how'? I was saying you have to be very observant. Big Daddy—most all stickmen, for that matter—was and are exceedingly skilled in slight of hand. They practice for hours perfecting it. You people were too busy placing bets, bitching and grumbling to one another to notice him make the switch. After the point was made, he simply went to the little pocket that wouldn't produce that number, palmed the dice, then made the switch when moving the hand over the straights to fiddle with a come bet. One clean, swift, normal-appearing stroke. Don't feel bad. You're not the first taken in by a slick stickman." Fargo glanced among the unsmiling faces. "Is the owner of the bank here?"

"Yes," a well-dressed man answered. "My name is Eldon Crabtree. I own the bank."

"Fine," Fargo replied. "Now, if all you local citizens will move up around the table—you too, Mr. Crabtree—I have something for you to hear. All you visitors can go gather at the bar. I'll get to you people in a few minutes. Drinks are on the house."

The out-of-towners sauntered grumbling to the bar. Fargo told the three saloon girls to get behind the bar and start pouring. He asked the banker, "Thurston keep his money in your bank?"

"Yes. Two accounts."

"How much in each?"

"I'm sorry, friend, but that's privileged information."

"Not anymore, it isn't," Fargo quickly replied. "Thurston stole it. Now we're going to give it back. How much?"

"I'm also the executor of his will," Crabtree persisted. "The man has a widow."

Fargo exhaled. Those around the table glowered at the banker. Fargo said, "Mr. Crabtree, I don't give a damn if he has six widows and ten kids, he still stole that money. One more time, how much is in the accounts?"

It wasn't necessary for Crabtree to be told that he could expect to see a line of townspeople formed outside his bank when he came to open it the next morning, ready to withdraw their funds. The banker capitulated under the hard stares. "Eight thousand in the Emporium account, $26,354.16 in his personal. Those amounts are as of the close of business today."

Fargo nodded. A few low whistles were heard. "Then I reckon any cash we find on the premises represents what he took in today. Is that a correct assumption?"

"Yes. Thurston always deposited the previous day's receipts the minute I opened the bank the next morning. I'd say whatever is here came in since this morning."

Again Fargo nodded, then looked at the faces in the gathering and picked out a local he knew. "Mr. Kaspar, why don't you pick two of these fine people to help you search Thurston's room, all of his belongings, then his office, if he has one. Bring every penny you find and put it on this table."

"Be damn glad to," Kaspar snorted. He pointed to

two men. "Come on, boys, we got work to do, damn interesting work."

After they left, Fargo selected five other men and told one, "Clean out the cash box at the bar. Don't forget to pick that bartender's pockets clean as a hound's tooth." He told the other four, "You men collect every cent on Thurston and his boys and put it on the table. Then take them outside and throw them in the mud." Looking toward the bar, he yelled, "Hey, Kid!" Half the men at the bar turned and looked expectantly at him. "You! The kid from Texas! I want you back over here!"

While waiting for the kid, Fargo asked the banker if he had pencil and paper.

Crabtree pulled his coat open and removed both from an inside pocket.

"Okay, gents," Fargo began, "line up and step to the table one at a time. Mr. Banker, you sit on the stool and take notes."

The line formed instantly. Fargo waved the first lucky man forward and told him, "State you name and tell the banker how much Thurston took you for since he came to town. If you lie and your neighbors find out, they'll shoot you dead."

The portly man gulped, leaned forward, and croaked, "Lyle Peabody. Four hunnert oughter do it for me."

"Louder, Mr. Peabody," Fargo said. "I want the others to hear your claim. Somebody will know if you're lying."

" 'Bout three hunnert an' fifty," Lyle shouted.

Fargo told him to go get a drink. When the banker looked up at Fargo and arched an eyebrow, Fargo said, "Put Peabody down for four hundred." He looked at the next eager face in the line. "Don't just stand there, man. It's payday in Walsenburg."

As those in line moved up and voiced claims, the men Fargo assigned to search Thurston, his henchmen, including the bartender, and raid the cash box began dumping money on the crap table, then went to the rear of the line.

Kaspar, excitement flooding his eyes, appeared at Fargo's side. "Found anything?" Fargo asked.

"Uh, huh. Come look."

Fargo followed him down the hall and through the door on the right side. The office was quite large and furnished without thought of expense. A big desk and comfortable chair were at the wall opposite the door. A matched pair of bloodred sofa chairs was between the desk and door. A fire burned in the stone hearth on Fargo's left.

Neil Kaspar pointed to it and asked, "Don't that beat all?"

Fargo took a second look. This time he saw what Kaspar meant. A life-size devil's head, horns and all, leered fiery red from the flames enveloping it. Fargo said, "It's cute, old man, but did you find any cash?"

One of the men helping Kaspar stepped to the desk, on which sat a wooden box. Opening the lid, he said, "It's in here. We didn't count it yet."

Kaspar added, "He slept across the hall. Didn't find nothing in there."

Fargo told the man holding the box lid open to bring the box and dump the contents on the crap table. They left and went to the alcove.

By the time the last claimant went before Crabtree, all of the gambler's money made a nice mound.

The banker struck a line below the last entry, quickly arrived at the sum, and said, "Looks like there's a little over fourteen thousand left in the combined accounts."

"Do you know of anyone else in town who lost to this man but isn't here?"

"Well, let's see . . . last week Voss mentioned what? A thousand, I believe he said. Maybe more. I know his wife is having to take in laundry. Millie Wilson is worried sick that Tom will learn she's lost eight hundred and fifty to Thurston. There's others—Fred Hushour being one—but I don't know how much he lost."

"Do you think five thousand would take care of those who weren't here tonight? How about any outstanding debt Thurston owed?"

"Oh, I'm positive five thousand would. Thurston paid cash for everything. He didn't owe anybody, and to the best of my knowledge nobody owes him. In that regard he was a fanatic, his one decent quality," Crabtree said.

"Okay, tomorrow morning you let everyone know they're going to get their money back. I'll tell these saloon girls and the pianist to drop by the bank also. Give each a couple of hundred. At least Thurston's been giving them free room and board. They'll make out. What does that leave us?"

"Nearly seven thousand."

Fargo thought briefly. "Does Walsenburg need anything?"

Crabtree's face brightened. "Yes, it does. A decent schoolhouse and a marm."

Freida Voss's schoolmarm bun flashed in Fargo's mind. "Will the seven thousand be enough?"

"More than enough."

"See that it happens. Mrs. Voss might be interested. If there's any money left, you keep it for services rendered." Fargo faced the crowded bar and shouted, "All right, gents, mosey over this way!" Glancing to the kid, he asked, "How about helping me maintain law and order?"

The kid cut the easy grin.

The crowd of men came with whiskeys in their hands and smiles on their faces. Fargo showed them the pile of money and said it was theirs. He told them, "There isn't going to be any fighting or squabbling over it. All of you are grown men. Act like it. Now, line up and come to the table one at a time. Collect what you lost this day. Not one penny more. Anybody raises hell or wants to argue about it, then me or the kid here will blow a hole in him."

As though Fargo had waved a magic wand, the line formed, with the end of it out on the porch. Fargo told the kid to get his losses first.

The young cowboy said, "I don't have any, mister. I don't come here to gamble."

Fargo looked at him anew, started to say something but headed for the bar instead. He went to the end of the bar closest to the double doors and rested a boot on the brass rail. The redhead came and poured him a beer, then filled another glass when the slim cowpuncher came and stood next to Fargo. Before either could speak, the four men appeared at the long side of the bar. One said, "None of us lost anything in here. But Douglas Thurston owes us four hundred dollars. We came to collect our money."

Fargo peered over the rim of his glass of beer into the man's sunken eyes. He heard the holstered Smith & Wesson's hammer cock. Lowering the glass, Fargo replied firmly, "Show the banker an IOU signed by Douglas Thurston and he'll give you your money."

The man slammed a fist down on the bartop. "We ain't got no goddamn IOU."

"Then you're out of luck. Lady, pour these men a drink before they leave."

As a unit they wheeled and strode through the swinging doors.

Fargo heard one of the double doors squeak one time too many. He shoved the kid one way and dodged in the other.

The loud gunshot fired behind him ripped through the saloon.

3

The bullet screamed a straight line where Fargo's back would have been, riffled the redhead's curly hair on the left side of her head, shattered the mirror as it ricocheted off, then buried itself in the back wall.

As it did, the Smith & Wesson barked. The lantern-jawed man standing with the one door open catapulted off the porch and hit hard in the mud.

The kid sprang for the doors. As he did, Fargo glanced at him and saw his lips were upturned at the corners.

The blonde watched the kid from Texas blast through the swinging doors, Fargo right behind him. The three men were mounted, bent low over their horse's necks and flying like the wind down the sloppy street, heading north. Both the Colt and Smith & Wesson threw hot lead at the hastily retreating forms.

"Let them go," Fargo suggested. "They aren't worth a night chase."

The cowboy quickly reloaded his gun. "I'll make sure they're gone." He unhitched the nearest horse and swung up in the saddle.

Fargo watched till the fast-riding cowboy disappeared in the black night, then went back inside. He stood at the near end of the bar and reloaded the Colt. He nodded for the redhead to come to him.

"Yeah, big man, what can I do for you?" Her dark-green eyes swept over his chest and powerful shoulders before settling on his chiseled face. Her glistening wide red lips formed into a provocative smile as she purred, "You can have anything you see, plus a few things you don't."

His lake-blue eyes were focused on the twin peaks trying to punch through the bodice of the flaming-red satin dress she wore. His gaze moved up to lock on hers. "What do they call you, honey?"

"Mazie. But I'm not lazy or crazy. Some mornings I wake up kinda hazy, though." She rested her elbows on the bartop and framed her pretty but freckled face in her soft-looking hands. The pose, intentional, offered him a nice view of her full breasts.

He shared a grin with her. "Been working here long?"

"I suppose I could lie and say this is my first day. Would you believe me?" When his head shook, she went on, "Didn't think you would. I'm—no, *we're* glad you killed that sorry bastard, Thurston, and the others. That no-count drifter too. Did you and the kid get his friends?"

"Hard to say. It's mighty dark out there. The kid's gone after them. Which room is yours?"

"Oh, boy," Mazie squealed, delighted, standing eagerly. "That mean I get your company tonight? You won't be sorry. It's at the top of the stairs, down the hall, second door on your right."

"If you behave and promise not to snicker. Go get ready for me. I'll be up soon as the kid comes back. I have to thank him for what he did."

"Well, just don't tarry. I'm already hot as a smoking pistol." Mazie blew him a kiss, turned, fetched a bottle from the shelf below the broken mirror, and sashayed toward the staircase.

Fargo sipped bourbon until the kid entered and came to stand beside him. Fargo handed the bottle to him. The kid took a swill, made a terrible face, shuddered, and handed it back.

Fargo was ready to believe that was the first liquor to pass over the kid's lips. The kid verified it when he said, "Dang, that stuff tastes horrible. Now I know why I never drank any before."

"Why did you?"

"Uh, er, I don't rightly know, mister." He looked at the amber bottle as though it might explode any second. "To knock the chill off, I guess. It's dadgummed chilly out there tonight. Is that stuff bourbon?"

"Yep. Acquire a taste for it and you'll never want any other kind. I appreciate you protecting my backside like you did. You drilled him right between the eyes best as I could tell."

"Should have. That's where I was thinking. I may have put a bullet in one of the others. He didn't fall from the saddle, but he screamed like he might be on fire. Sorry, mister, but it was too dark and mighty slippery out there." He seemed disgusted with his performance.

Fargo said, "You did good. What's your name, anyhow, and how young are you?"

The young man blushed. "Roy, sir. Roy Ballas. All the boys back at the Bar Z Bar call me Kid Ballas, though. I'm twenty going on twenty-one. Okay if I ask your name?"

"Sure. It's Fargo."

Kid Ballas stiffened. Beaming, he asked, "Not Skye Fargo, the Trailsman?"

"One and same. How'd you know my first name? The hotel register?"

"Well, I'll be danged! Skye Fargo standing right here." Roy pulled a fat envelope from inside his shirt and laid it on the bartop in front of Fargo. "Mr. Hollis—he owns the Bar Z Bar, or did I already mention that?—sent me to find and give this to you. Dangnation, now I can go back and say I saw Skye Fargo send a bunch of crooked gamblers to early graves. Mr. Hollis and the boys are going to be proud of me."

Fargo picked up the envelope and felt its weight on his palm. "What's in it, Kid?"

"Shucks, I don't know. Mr. Hollis sealed it."

Fargo had a good idea what he'd find inside: money and a letter asking him to go on a mission. Tapping the edge of the envelope on top of the bar, he inquired, "Before I open this and look, you want to tell me what you think I'll find?"

"Aw, shucks, Mr. Fargo, I don't know exactly, but I'd be willing to bet it has something to do with them taking her off."

"Who?"

"Two men. Never saw them myself, but—"

"I meant her."

"Oh, Jennie. She's Mr. and Mrs. Hollis' girl."

"All right. What about the men who took her?"

"Like I was saying, I never saw them. None of us did, except Mrs. Hollis, and the girl, of course. It happened two months ago. Oh, it was a most terrible stormy night. Lot of lightning and wind, rain whipping in almost parallel to the ground, and thunder booming, all but knocking over the bunkhouse where I was at, dressing my tack and all.

"They rode out of all that and went straight to the big house. Mrs. Hollis, good soul that she is, let them in. She fixed them a hot meal and everything. Jennie heard them talking and came down to see who it was. They left the next morning before any of us hands woke up. They took Jennie with them. I don't know much more than that. Mrs. Hollis wouldn't talk to any of us about it. I could tell by her eyes and the way she acted, wringing her hands and all, that she wanted to, but she kept her mouth shut and cried."

"And Mr. Hollis?"

"He wasn't there. Mr. Hollis and most of the men were driving a herd of longhorns to the stockyards in Cowtown. He didn't know till they came back. The very same day he called me to the big house and gave me that envelope and two hundred dollars for expenses while I was gone. He ordered me not to come back till I found you."

"Where is the Bar Z Bar, exactly?"

"About twenty miles west of Estelline, up near the bottom of the Texas Panhandle, near Childress."

"Okay, Kid Ballas, you can ride back and report that you found me. Tell your boss and his wife that I'll do what I can for them. You winged one, huh?"

"Yes, sir. I'm pretty dang sure he's got a sore spot on him someplace." He blushed again, this time shaking his head, all as though he was embarrassed for being a poor shot, which he wasn't.

Fargo looked at the blonde and brunette standing behind the bar near the far end. Both were eyeing them hopefully, if not hungrily. "I have one waiting for me upstairs," Fargo explained. "You want one of those two? The slim brunette looks as though she knows how to break broncs bareback."

Kid Ballas inspected his fingernails. "Shucks, Mr. Fargo," he muttered, "I haven't learned how yet."

Fargo laid a palm on Roy's forearm and squeezed tenderly. In a fatherly tone he advised, "Yeah, well, Kid, when you do, be fast to put it in the holster, damn slow to draw it out." He winked and strolled toward the stairs.

Fargo rapped once on Mazie's door and entered. Light-blue curtains, flimsy and floor-length, hid the single window. A lamp burned on the nightstand next to her bed. The fresh scent of cleanliness drifted in the heady aroma present in most ladies' boudoirs. Fargo suspected the scent came from the sheets she had obviously put on the bed. The creases of the folds still showed. She had drawn the sheet up and tucked it under her chin. Long flowing bright-red hair surrounded her inquisitive face and disappeared beneath the sheet. The dark-green eyes angled on him fairly gleamed with anticipation. And she was smiling.

Fargo came and sat on the edge of the bed to pull off his boots. She raised, curled a slender soft arm around his neck, and pressed the side of her face against his muscled broad back. He half-turned and pulled her around to face him. For an instant she looked almost childlike: upturned face, spellbound expression, wondering eyes, holding her breath. He lowered his open mouth to kiss her lips. The subdued appearance and pose he'd seen a second ago vanished in that instant, replaced just as quickly by hunger, the likes he'd never been subjected to before.

Mazie was all over him, writhing, squirming, and her arms, hands, and long legs were clutching, encircling, and hugging him, not tenderly, but wantonly, as though he was the first and might be the last. Her open mouth fused to his, and she moaned at first taste. "Uhmmnn . . . oh, Jesus, Jesus, Jesus, yes," she whimpered. Her hot tongue worked furiously inside his mouth, tried to capture his, could not, and settled for caressing the tender membrane.

She kicked the sheet off the bed, got on her knees behind him, and started kissing his neck and ears, moaning and whimpering all the time. "Please, big man . . . oh,

God, I'm hot." One of her hands slipped inside the waist of his Levi's, slid down, and curled around his member. She gasped, "Oh, my God . . . oh, my God . . . I'm so lucky, so lucky."

Fargo withdrew the reluctant hand and stood. She collapsed on the bed. Her hair cascaded to the floor and both hands reached out, the slender fingers trying vainly to grab and bring him back to her. "Whoa, Mazie. Just hold it a damn minute." He danced away from the finger-tentacles. "Damn," he sighed, "you're no slowpoke."

Mazie flopped onto her stomach and leaned her head over the edge of the bed. "Give it to me," she gasped. Her eyelids were down and her lips parted sensuously. Her breaths came in quick jerks, bounced her pillowy breasts. "What's taking you so long? Oh, God . . . I think I felt an orgasm."

Fargo still had his boots on. The gun belt too. He unbuckled and swung it off while eyeing the fluff of bushy hot-red hair in the V of her parted legs. He moved to the only chair in the room, an armless rocker, and laid the gun belt on the seat. Bracing himself with one hand on the backrest, he started pulling off a boot, watching Mazie all the time.

When she opened her eyes and didn't see him, she crawled off the bed, rushed to the door, and opened it, lamenting most disgustedly, "Damn! He got away! Shit, Mazie, you did it again!"

"I'm over here." He chuckled.

She shut the door and spun around in the same movement. A renewed happiness flooded her face. She hurried to help him undress.

"Take it easy," he cautioned. "Don't pop those buttons off."

"I won't," she replied.

Fargo couldn't remember the last time all his buttons were undone this fast. If Mazie didn't know anything else, she did know how to undress a man in record time. Tits bounced and flopped as she pulled his shirt off and tossed it at a corner. The neckerchief was flung toward the window. Then the Levi's were yanked down, pulled off, and sent flying. She all but ripped his underdrawers in her near panic to get them down and off. They fell near the shirt.

The bed was too far away for Mazie. She swept the gun belt off the rocker seat and gulped, "Sit, big man. Spread your knees." He moved too slow for the hellcat. Mazie pushed him down in the seat, dropped to her knees, and pulled his apart.

Her widened eyes riveted on his hard manhood. The fingers on both her hands wrapped around it. She gulped and licked her lips as she bent them to the blood-swollen summit peaking through the tight sheath of foreskin. Fargo entwined his fingers in her hair and coaxed her to proceed. The crown entered. He felt her lips tighten, the thin sheath slide down, then stop when the lips relaxed for the downward plunge. She gurgled around it. "Oh, oh, so nice . . . so nice."

She set her head in motion, rolling, bobbing and yawing, the pace governed somewhat by his tugs and guidance with her hair. Her hands roamed over his hard belly, fondled and squeezed the muscles of his chest and arms. And she moaned deliriously, savoring him, hard muscles, throbbing organ and all . . . until Fargo pulled her head back.

She stared into his lake-blue eyes. He saw joy in hers. Her mouth was open and the soft tongue circled the moist lips. Her breaths were long as she filled her lungs for what was yet to come. He would accommodate her. "I love you, big man," she whispered. "Oh, God, how I love you."

Fargo realized those words uttered with passion, her kneeling between his knees, the delight she had given him, the catching of her breath, were all but a prelude, the calm before the storm. He would, at least, choose where it happened, the lightning in her, his thunder, their clashing of flesh. He began by taking her upper arms and slowly lifting her to stand. Shifting his gaze to her breasts, he nudged her legs apart and coaxed her to straddle the rocker as she came to him.

His lips parted. She fed the left nipple between them. He nibbled on it, swished his tongue around the areola, then sucked in all of the soft breast his mouth could hold.

Mazie's head lolled, her eyes closed; she curled an arm around his neck and drew him tight, gasping, "Harder . . . suck harder . . . don't be afraid . . . oh, Jesus, that's good . . . you won't hurt me."

Fargo slid his lips to the other breast, took in the nipple and areola, then buried his face in the pillowy mound of warm flesh. Mazie screamed, "Aaaeeeyyiii! Oh, God!" He felt her body shudder and then her fingernails dig into his back. She writhed, murmuring, "Yes, yes . . . oh, Jesus, yes . . . I'm on fire, burning . . . Aaah, aaah, oh, God, don't stop."

Her stance positioned her lower lips to touch his crown, and when she moved, they dragged across it. She was hot, all right. He could feel the moist heat generated by her lower charms and the tinglings of her pubic hairs each time one grazed his sensitive summit. Combined, they aroused him greatly.

Moving back to the left breast, he grasped her hips and urged her to lower and take him in. She eagerly obeyed, squirming gently to help it part the swollen lips, then let them surround him and forced the penetration by squatting suddenly. "Aaaaeeeiii . . . aaaaeeeiii!" she screamed. "Oh, my God."

He lifted her knees and urged her to bend them to ride down his torso. She did and held on, keeping her balance with her hands clasped behind his neck. The jackknifed squatting position permitted extra-deep penetration, and it came with considerable grunts and moans from her. Fargo set the rocker in motion.

"Aaaeeeiii," she screamed. "Oh, Jesus . . . yes, yes, yes! More, big man, give me all of it . . . faster, Jesus, go faster!" She screamed anew, "Aaaeeeiii . . . harder!"

Now her hips were swinging and rocking, pumping hard and fast, gyrating, shoving down hard. Sweat rolled off both of them. They sucked in breaths, gasped, took in more. Mazie let go of him, pulled his hands from her hips, and swiveled around to lean her back on his chest. In the new position, she spread her long legs, reached up, curled both hands behind his neck, and began bouncing up and down wildly, screaming joyously, "That's it! That's it, big man! Give it to me . . . please don't ever stop."

Fargo cupped both breasts in his hands and squeezed with the erect nipples poked between his fingers. Her back arched. Her body trembled. She screamed, "Now! Now, big man! Oh, God . . . please come with . . . Aaaeeeiii!"

Her contraction was one of the strongest he'd ever felt. It milked, tightened, squeezed even more. There was no stopping it. Fargo's stomach sucked in, his buttock cheeks tensed. He closed his eyes and erupted in jolting spurts. Mazie moaned, "Oh, Jesus Christ . . . yes, yes . . . so hot, so very hot. Give it all to me. I want it all. Oh, God . . . I see shooting stars. They're so beautiful, so bright." Her hands went to his knees. She bent forward, got solid footholds on the floor, then pumped furiously, wiggling her rump in all directions as she did.

Slowly the rocker stopped. She fell limp back against his muscled chest, her slender arms dangling nearly to the floor. Fargo felt himself limbering, and so did she. Mazie made a few movements to bring it back up, but one was too generous and he slipped out.

Breathing hard, she leaned to one side and looked at him through half-drooped eyelids, smiling her satisfaction. He kissed her openmouthed. All the fight was gone from her. She made a feeble attempt to devour his lips, tongue, and mouth, but she was too weak and exhausted. The best she could do was give him a wet kiss in return.

Fargo used a finger to move strands of her hair from the sweat covering her chest and shoulders and work them to her back. It was quiet now. She cuddled in his arms with her head snuggled in the crook of his shoulder. Again she whispered, "I love you, big man. Oh, God, how I love you."

4

Mazie Freeman's sleepy green eyes opened slowly. As they did, her peaceful, fully satisfied face awakened a soft smile. One hand slid down to caress what had given her enormous pleasure followed by the best night's sleep she'd had in months—and found only the sheet. A hint of panic swept through her. The hand groped all down the bed as her eyes widened fully awake.

Fargo stood at her window. The early-morning sunlight spilled through it and on the rancher's letter he held for reading. Noticing that she was awake and in a quandary about something—her left hand was searching frantically beneath the top sheet—he said, " 'Morning, Mazie."

"Oh, God," she answered, rolling over quickly. "I thought you were gone."

"Nope. Been reading." He jiggled the letter.

She saw he was dressed, including the gun belt. "You're leaving? So soon? You were going to show—"

His chuckle cut her query short. "Woman, I showed you how five different tribes of Indians bed-wrestle before you, not me, called it quits."

"I know," she mewed. "Does that mean—"

"No," he interrupted. "We'll get to the Navajos next time."

"Next time?" Mazie left the bed, bringing the sheet with her. Pulling it around her nakedness, she came to him. "When will that be?"

He looked at Hollis' letter again. "Don't rightly know. A Texas rancher has a job for me."

"Aw, oh, my God! Not in Texas. You're not going there, are you? It's hot as hell in Texas. Stay here with me . . . please stay, tell me you will. Please?"

Fargo chuckled, not because she wanted him, but because of her pout. Mazie looked destroyed. "No, honey, I'm not going to Texas. I don't know where I'm going, but it won't be there." Turning serious, he said, "This letter is from Richard Hollis, who owns the Bar Z Bar. It says, 'Mr. Fargo, on July twentieth two unsavory men took my little girl, Jennie, as their hostage when they left my home. They told Alice—she's my wife and the mother of our sweet daughter—that if she put the law on them they would kill my Jennie. They said they would turn her loose somewhere in Colorado if they knew no law was after them.

" 'Those two men talked when they didn't think Mrs. Hollis could hear. She was in the kitchen at the time. But she heard them say they needed to get to Saint Lucifer fast, that the law would never find them there. None of us ever heard of such a place. Maybe you have.

" 'We want our daughter back. I'm sending one of my ranch hands to find you. Roy Ballas is his name. Don't let his size or looks fool you. Kid's gentle, all right, until he gets riled. He is dependable and trustworthy. If you need him, you have my permission.

" 'You have found the five hundred dollars in the envelope. Use it for expenses. I'll give you another five hundred upon Jennie's safe return home. I'm calling on you, Mr. Fargo, because you are the very best. Please help us. Thank you.' It's signed Richard and Alice Hollis.'' Fargo lowered the letter and gazed into Mazie's upturned face. Her eyes were watery. A tear fell from each as he said, "So you see, I don't know where I'm going." He cupped her face in his hands and wiped the tears away with his thumbs.

She sniffled, "Saint Lucifer, Saint—where, when did I hear that? I know I did." Fargo watched her frown, then her face brighten. "Come on," she chirped, "let's go roll Vera and Frances out of bed. We once talked about a Lucifer." Mazie slipped free of his hands and headed for the door. Over her shoulder she said, "The sooner you find her, the sooner you'll be back in my bed, between my thighs."

Fargo followed her down the hall to a door. He waited outside while she went in and made the angry whore get up and dress. "Come down in the saloon," Mazie's voice said. "He won't even miss you."

She breezed past Fargo, shot him a wink, and went to the adjoining room. "Goddammit, Vera, I said get up," he heard her snap. "This is more important than lying in bed with that smelly cowboy. Put something on and come downstairs. Now, Vera!"

Mazie came out with her eyes rolled back. "They'll be down in a minute, big man. Why don't you wait at the bar? I'll throw a dress on and be right down."

He nodded and headed for the stairs.

Except for the scarecrow still draped on the poker table, the saloon was deserted, but it looked as though most of the horses were still hitched and waiting outside. Fargo imagined their riders scattered in rooms throughout Walsenburg, snoozing off drunkenness. Damn, he thought, I forgot to give my clothes to Mrs. Voss. Maybe later.

The blonde appeared on the top landing. She wore a long checked shirt that obviously belonged to the man asleep in her bed, and baggy drawers tied above the knees with yellow ribbons. She looked as though she might have wrestled half the king's army during the night, and lost.

" 'Morning, ma'am," Fargo offered.

She yawned, scratching her butt, and started down the stairs. At the bottom she walked over and braced herself against the bar across from Fargo. Soft-blue pupils surrounded by tiny red spiderwebs studied his face. Though her face was morning-haggard, he believed she could be no more than twenty years old. Scratching her left breast, she observed, "How come you don't look all frazzled out? Mazie losing her touch?"

Before he could answer, Mazie and the leggy brunette appeared on the top landing. Mazie had slipped on a short brown dress that had a bright-yellow hem. The brunette had on a pair of jeans and a white sleeveless shirt. She looked as though she had fought the other half of the army. If so, Fargo thought, she may have put up one hell of a fight. They came down and stood beside the blonde. Seeing the brunette up close, Fargo changed his mind and decided she too had taken an ass-whipping. She looked worse off than the blonde.

Mazie said, "This is Frances, big man. Say, what's your name, anyhow?"

"Fargo."

The blonde's eyes kicked up. "No shit? You're really him? Skye Fargo, the one they call the Trailsman?"

He nodded.

"I heard about you," the blonde claimed rather excitedly. She cut the bloodshot eyes to Mazie. "You lucky bitch." She glanced back to Fargo. "My name's Vera. Ever hear of me?" He shook his head. "Before I came here, I helped out for a while in Miss Dolly's saloon. She told me all about you—and I do mean all. Damn, and to think you were in my sights last night. I get all the lousy luck."

"Yeah, well," he began, "maybe some other time we can change your luck. Right now Mazie says the three of you heard, talked about a place called—"

"Saint Lucifer," Mazie hastened to interrupt. "Remember?"

Frances stared twin stilettos through slitted hazel eyes at Mazie. "You made me crawl out of bed to talk about that? Goddamn, Mazie Freeman, you—"

"Tell me what you know about Saint Lucifer," Fargo directed, "then you can go crawl back in it."

"Who mentioned it?" Mazie asked, looking at Frances. "You or Vera?"

Vera ran her fingers through her mop of tangled honey-blond hair and sighed, "I did. Thurston made me screw one of the drifters. That particular time was a couple of months back. You know, he's the one who shot a man after he said the drifter was cheating in cards."

"Uh, huh, I remember now," Frances agreed. "He got real drunk after he killed the guy."

"Yeah," Vera verified, "too drunk to stay on top. I had to get on him."

"And he went to sleep," Mazie helped her remember.

"And he went to sleep," Vera echoed. "Never was so relieved in all my life. Hell, he didn't have the equipment to dig with if he'd been stone-cold sober." She paused and glanced at Fargo. "Anyhow, I laid there and listened to him mumbling something about this Saint Lucifer. 'Gotta get to Saint Lucifer before they catch me,' he kept repeating. Over and over he said that. I jabbed an elbow in his ribs and asked where Saint Lucifer was."

"And?" Fargo pressed.

"Northwest is what I heard."

"Hmm," Fargo mused. "Northwest can be near or far, and it's damn sure wide."

"Tell him what else the drifter said," Mazie encouraged.

Vera said, "He had his face mashed down in the pillow, so I didn't hear too good or all of what he said. It was something about meeting the boys there. It was, you know, sketchy. I heard 'running from the law' a couple of times."

Mazie shifted weight to the other foot. "Fargo, now that I think on it, most of the drifters who came here and got money from Thurston rode west when they left."

Fargo mentally noted the drifters who got away last night had turned west onto Dynamite Street.

Frances added an observation of her own. "She's right, Fargo. Tell you something else too, something I ain't told nobody, not even the girls here."

"Well, you sorry—"

Fargo butted into Mazie's forming accusation. "Let Frances finish."

"Thank you, mister. As I was saying"—she cut her eyes at Mazie—"I overheard Thurston tell two of them drifters at different times that he'd send word to Russell at Saint Lucifer when it was time for them to come back. That sounds like he meant all of them. What do you think, Fargo?"

"I agree." A myriad thoughts, all bad, collided in his brain. One of the thoughts dominated the others. He voiced it. "Sounds to me like Douglas Thurston's been assembling a gang of desperadoes, lawbreakers, killers, and what not in this Saint Lucifer. My guess is, he planned to bring them back and take over Walsenburg. Owning Walsenburg and controlling it are two different things. I think once he owned and controlled Walsenburg, he intended to use it as a base for plundering near and far."

Mazie volunteered, "A Texas rancher wants him to find his little girl. The rancher said two men stole her and said they'd let her go somewhere in Colorado. I don't recall any drifters having a girl with them, or a woman for that matter. Do you, Vera? Huh, Frances?"

Both whores shook their heads.

Vera added, "Not one."

"That doesn't mean they didn't," Frances suggested. "They could have parked their women at—"

Fargo was beginning to like Frances' fast mind. He completed her suggestion, "The Buckhorn. You girls have been a big help. Now you can go back to bed." He winked at Mazie.

"Naw, hell, I'm wide awake now," Frances said, giving Fargo a suggestive look.

Fargo chuckled and shook his head. "No, honey, maybe next time. I've got work to do." He came around the bar and headed for the double doors.

Going through them, he heard Vera ask, "Is that a promise?"

He grinned and shook his head a few times while crossing over to the Buckhorn.

Freida Voss greeted him with a cool brown stare from where she stood behind the registration counter. "Sir, I owe you one dollar or a wash and ironing. Which do you prefer?"

"The latter. Give me a few minutes. You will find my clothes out in the hall by my door." He started up the stairs, paused to turn, and asked, "Is there any chance you can get the café to fix and bring me a breakfast?"

"Of course they will, Mr. Fargo. They do it all the time. What would you like?"

"Four eggs fixed any way. Some bacon, biscuits, and a pot of hot coffee."

"They have the best grape jelly in these parts. It's the one decent thing that hussy can do."

"Some of the jelly too. My stuff will be in the hall, ma'am." He touched the brim of his hat and climbed the stairs.

The gun belt was draped over the back of a chair, the Colt tucked under his pillow, and the clothes left outside his door. Fargo stretched out naked on the bed, drew the sheet up to his chest, and stared deep in thought at the ceiling. The more he pondered it, the more assured he felt that Saint Lucifer would prove out to be a secret name for more than an ordinary town. Saint Lucifer would be a collection point, without question a haven for thieves and murderers. It was probably a hastily thrown together encampment of shanties made from boughs. Desperadoes, especially those on the run, weren't noted for building decent places to live. They made do with whatever was handy: barns, caves, lean-tos, and the like.

In all likelihood their nerves were strained to the breaking point due to the self-imposed isolation. Crooks were a restless lot. Moreover, each thought he was bigger and tougher than the next man. Fargo decided they probably argued and fought over who would run things, be the boss of Saint Lucifer. He wondered about that until a gentle knock on his door moved his hand under the pillow. He cocked the Colt and said, "Come in. The door's unlocked."

He watched the knob twist. The door parted a few inches. Millie Wilson bumped it open with her rump and backed in. She held a platter of steaming food in one hand, the bail of a coffeepot in the other. A porcelain coffeecup hung by its handle crooked in the index finger at the bail. A smile was on her face and her curious eyes on the lump at his crotch where he held the Colt. He raised the barrel and uncocked the weapon. The movement put a peak in the sheet.

Millie gulped. Her pupils grew quite large and excited. He lowered the barrel quickly and said, "Come on in, Mrs. Wilson. I don't bite. Put everything on top of the bureau. How's Mr. Wilson this morning? That coffee smells good."

Millie kept her gaze on the sheet while crossing to the bureau. He kept his on her charming butt, the cheeks of which looked as though they wanted out of the thin off-white dress that hid nothing. "Tom's feeling poorly this morning. I'm handling the café all by myself. Want me to fill the cup?"

"Please do." He watched her pour. "Seen Kid Ballas this morning?"

"No. It's a mite early for him to be out. He stays at the Hunsuckers' place. Johanna fixes breakfast for him. Want me to feed you? I will." Her gaze, still on the sheet, conveyed much hope.

"Not when the lady's husband is down sick."

"Aw, Tom, he ain't *that* sick. I said he was feeling poorly. His fat gut's giving him trouble . . . again."

"I've changed my mind. Bring the food and coffeecup over here. You sit on the edge of the bed while I eat and we chat."

Millie quickly complied. He rearranged the pillow and propped his back against it and the headboard. The edge of the sheet drew down to his navel during the movement. She braced erect when he brought the Colt from beneath it and laid the gun next to his waist. He took the plate of food from her and started eating. Between bites he indicated for her to give him a sip of coffee.

"Have you ever heard of Saint Lucifer?" he asked around a bite of eggs.

Her curly black hair shook. "I don't think . . . No! I did hear that name. Not directly. Tom did. He told me."

Fargo munched on a biscuit laden with butter and grape jelly. "Did Tom say who mentioned it?"

"Uh, a drifter, I think it was."

"How long ago?"

"Oh, gosh, when was it? A month, maybe six weeks ago. I forget, exactly. Could've been longer than that."

"Was the drifter a customer?"

"Yes. Two of them came in for lunch. Tom gave me hell, again, for stepping out of the kitchen to have a look at them. Fussed at me, I should say. I can't help it if I have a good-looking hiney."

"Uh, huh," Fargo muttered, "and a wild bosom to go with it."

"Did you say you wanted to see my bosom?" Her hands leapt to the buttons of her shirt.

"No, no, I didn't. I said give me another sip. What did they say about your . . . your fine butt, that is?"

"Sir, are you making fun of me?"

"No, you're the one who said you have a good-looking

ass. All I did was agree. What did they say about it that made Tom fuss at you?"

"If you want to believe Tom, one remarked to the other, 'Russell would take that filly's ass away from us if we took her to Saint Lucifer with us.' According to Tom, the other drifter snickered, 'Yeah, we'll give him the little blond girl. We'll be tired of her ass by then, anyhow.'"

"Think carefully now. They did say girl? Not woman?"

"That's what Tom told me. A blond girl."

"Six weeks ago?"

"More or less. You sure you don't want me to slip under that sheet with you? It's sorta chilly in here."

"Not this time, honey. Mazie Freeman's done wore me out."

"That long-legged bitch? What's she got that I haven't?"

Fargo chuckled. "You need to go to the bank when it opens. The banker has something nice for you."

Millie's brow furrowed. "What?"

"Your gambling losses to Thurston."

"Oh, how'd you hear about that? Mazie Freeman's big mouth?"

"No. Word gets around. I heard after I shot and killed Thurston last night."

She stammered, "You, you shot and killed him?"

Fargo nodded and handed her the empty platter. "Him and his cronies."

"I'll be damned," she muttered. "Good for you. Thurston had me by the short hairs and was twisting a knot in them. He said if I didn't pay up, starting tomorrow, I was going to have to put out to him and his drifter pals. You have saved my ass, mister."

"Yes, well, get out of here and go back to the café. You'll hear all about it from your customers." He shot her a Fargo wink.

She stood and looked down at his bunch-up, shook her head, said, "That looks mighty good," then forced herself to go to the door. Opening it, she said, "Mister, I owe you. We all do. And I pay my debts . . . one way or another."

"Maybe I'll collect someday. If you see Kid Ballas, tell him I'm looking for him."

While staring at the ceiling again, he heard her leave and close the door. If Tom heard correct, he thought, then Saint Lucifer will prove to be a hellhole.

Now it looked as though Fargo would have to deal with captured women forced into slavery, and God only knew to what extent, as well as dangerous men hiding from the law, and Satan only knew how many. The name "Lucifer" certainly applied. Fargo couldn't fit "Saint" into it. He napped off trying to.

Ben Voss's voice saying, "Mr. Fargo, I have your clothes," snapped Fargo's eyes open.

He got up and parted the door. Ben smiled as he passed the folded garments in to Fargo. They smelled fresh and clean. "Tell your wife I appreciate this. The Buckhorn's got my business every time I come to town. By the way, Ben, drop by the bank when it opens. Crabtree has something for you."

Ben nodded. "Yes, I heard. Thank you."

"All in a night's work," Fargo replied. He shut the door. Within seconds he was dressed and had the gun belt strapped on, striding for the door. In the lobby, he asked the Vosses where the printer's shop was located.

Freida Voss answered, "Certainly. Go past the cross street. You will see it on your right. Walsenburg *Star-Gazette* is between the general store and the jail. The Schuttes own it."

Fargo moseyed up the street, now solid with gooey mud. Walsenburg was in the throes of waking up and in the process of drying out. A few of the shopkeepers, those who had a boardwalk out front, were busy cleaning dirty streaks off their front windows. Coming to the intersection, Fargo spotted a big black mare pulling a fine buggy of the same color. The banker, Crabtree, held the reins. Except for his white shirt, he wore all black. He waved toward the buggy and kept trudging along in the mud.

A short man, half-bald already and clearly not yet having enjoyed his thirty-fifth birthday, sat at a badly scarred rolltop desk on the other side of a waist-high counter supported by round wooden uprights. The fencelike barrier separated the customers from the working area of the print shop. There was a swinging door in the middle of the barrier, which ran across the entire width of the room. On it were two small stacks of paper. The place smelled of ink.

" 'Morning," Fargo said as he stepped to the counter.

The man leaned back in his squeaky chair, swiveled to face his customer, and peered over the rims of small eyeglasses. "Good morning to you. May we be of service?"

"Hope so. Do you do posters?"

"Of course." He pushed back and came to stand at the counter. Sliding the top sheet off a stack of paper, he added smiling, "Lowest prices in town. That's because we're the only printers. What kind of a poster, Mr.—"

"Fargo. I need a wanted-dead-or-alive poster. Can you fix me up with one? I believe your name is Schutte?" Fargo extended his hand.

Schutte's grip was firm. "Yes, it is. John's the first name. Yes, we can supply that order, odd though it is." John glanced over his shoulder and called out, "Malva! Drop what you're doing and come up front. Customer needs a wanted." He looked back at his tall customer and explained, "Malva makes the wood etchings. She's gifted."

A rather pretty woman, slightly younger than John Schutte, appeared from behind a high stack of wood crates. She was trim of build and wore an ink-smeared apron to protect her gingham dress. She approached wiping her hands on the apron. "Good morning, sir," she greeted cheerily in a tiny voice. "What do you need?"

Fargo watched her draw a sheet of blank paper the exact width of the counter from the other stack. She removed a long sharp-pointed pencil from where it rode on her left ear hidden by brown tresses. "I want it of me," he told her.

Schutte tensed. Frowning, he said, "I understood you to say dead or alive."

"You heard right," Fargo answered. "I have my reasons."

"Of course," Malva replied easily, as though the request was made all the time. "Come inside and sit in that chair"—she pointed to a straight-back beside a table having a tilted top—"and I'll make a drawing of you. John, why don't you pour us some coffee."

Fargo pushed through the swinging door and went to the chair. Malva rested more than sat on the stool to face her subject. She smoothed the sheet of paper on the tabletop and started the sketch. "Please keep your head perfectly still, sir. You may move your eyes until I say to stop."

From upside down he watched her draw his head, then sketch in his features, hat, and neckerchief. John arrived with two steaming cups of coffee while she was heavying up Fargo's eyebrows. She paused and turned the drawing for him to see. After taking a sip of the brew, she asked, "What do you think? Do you like it?"

"Remarkable," he muttered. "You might put a scared look in my eyes, though. Can you fake that?"

"Sure, I can. Anything else?"

"No, that should do it." He swallowed about half his cup of coffee.

Malva went back to work on the portrait. Fifteen minutes later she held it for him to view.

Fargo grinned and nodded. "No question about it, ma'am, that's me."

"Fine. How much do we say you are worth dead or alive, and to who and where, and what heinous crime did you commit?"

Fargo gave her questions brief thought. "Two thousand ought to stir interest. Say for murder. Make it cold-blooded. Who and where?"

"We need a sheriff," she coaxed.

Fargo grinned. "Yeah, why not?" he mused. "I'm wanted by Sheriff Roy Ballas, right here in Walsenburg."

John's chair squeaked when he swiveled around and stared at Fargo.

Surprised, Malva glanced up at Fargo. "Kid Ballas? Mister, he's too young and sweet. Since when did he become our sheriff?"

Fargo chuckled. "The really tough ones usually are sweethearts. As for him being sheriff, I just made him it. The people who will see this poster won't know he isn't.

That's what counts. How soon can you have it printed and ready for me?"

"We'll get right on it. John, do you know of any reason why we can't have it ready for him shortly after noon?"

Without looking up from his paperwork, John shook his head.

Fargo stood and nodded. "Perfect. I'll see you sometime after lunch. Good day, ma'am." He touched the brim of his hat, turned, and walked outside.

At the intersection he heard Neil Kaspar cussing a blue streak inside his stable up Dynamite Street. Fargo angled that way and fought the mud while going to the livery. Upon entering the stable, Fargo saw Kaspar standing in the alleyway with his back to him. Before Fargo could speak, Kaspar drew back a booted foot and kicked a horse apple clean to the far wall, hollering, "Son of a bitch" for the umpteenth time.

"Whoa, old man," Fargo said in a pleasant tone. "You're going to bust a blood vessel."

Kaspar spun around and with the toe of the boot kicked a clod of mud from the alleyway. His face gleamed beet-red and his eyes were blazing just as crimson. "I hope I do," he growled. "Whut cha want, anyhow? I ain't got time. Your horse is okay."

"Hold on, Kaspar. Just hold on a damn minute and simmer down."

"Simmer down? Simmer down?" He stabbed a finger skyward, pumped the arm a few times. "Look at that," he bellowed, then dropped the arm and pointed to the ground behind him. "And that! Hell, no, I ain't simmering down."

Fargo glanced up. A big hole gaped in the roof. He looked behind Kaspar. Several horses stood in a quagmire of horse manure, ugly black mud, and water with hay floating on top. It covered a wide low spot at the far end of the building.

"That Swede bastard's gonna charge me a flat hunnert dollars to fix that damn roof. Shit!" He yanked his beat-up hat off and slammed it onto the ground, then kicked it toward the entrance. "What is it? I'm busy."

"Uh, well, why don't I come back after you get over the mad spell?"

Kaspar's shoulders sagged. A terrible sigh gushed from his snarled lips. Deflated, he became as civil as Neil Kaspar could get. "Naw, hell, this mess ain't going nowhere. After all you done for me—us! The whole damn town . . . What can I do for you?"

"You think you can take your mind off that hole in the roof, that mess, long enough for us to have a little talk?"

Kaspar grinned. "What hole?"

Fargo gestured for them to move into the entranceway. He preferred standing in the sunlight and out of the smelly odor rising off the quagmire. "I was wondering if you ever heard of Saint Lucifer. Have you?"

Kaspar rolled his eyes back, scratched in his beard, and replied, "Saint Louis and Saint Joe, yes, but Saint Lucifer, no. Where is it?"

"I was hoping you'd tell me."

"Important?" Kaspar's expression instantly became sheepish. He answered his own question. "That was a dumb thing for me to say. Of course it's important. If it wasn't you wouldn't have asked."

"Drifters have mentioned it."

"Drifters, huh? Well, mister, you saw how it goes 'tween me and them no-count drifters. I don't talk to them 'less it's to run 'em off."

"I'm told some ride west when leaving."

"That's true." He retrieved and put on his hat. "Pass right by going to the main trail. Don't speak, though. I wouldn't answer if they did."

Fargo knew the trail west was bisected by others leading north or south. He was fixing their junctures in his mind when the old man mentioned, "They go to Carter's Creek."

Carter's Creek was about a day's ride west. "Oh, I thought . . . How do you know that, old man?"

"Cooney O'Leary told me. Cooney's the smithy at Carter's Creek. Big son of a bitch. Strong as a team of oxen. He comes to Walsenburg every once in a while to pay a visit to those saloon girls. Me and him, we talk."

The walk through the mud had been worth the effort.

At least Fargo now knew the drifters didn't branch off the main trail after leaving Walsenburg. They apparently continued on to Alamosa, maybe as far as Creede. "Thanks, Neil. You've been of help. Maybe Swede won't charge that much."

"Oh, yes, he will." The old man apparently knew the town carpenter well. Fargo suspected the two had run-ins before.

Fargo touched the brim of his hat and stepped out into the black goo. During the brief time he'd been inside the livery, the street had become active. Several buggies and one-horse farm wagons were parked at the bank. Farther down two heavy-geared mountain wagons were moving toward him. A farm wagon stood outside the feed store. Passing slowly in front of the hotel was a long-haul wagon laden with feed sacks. It looked as though it might bog down in the mud any second.

Fargo glanced toward the bank again. He presumed the word had spread like a prairie fire that Douglas Thurston was dead and his spoils being returned by Crabtree. He headed that way.

When he passed by, Fargo looked inside through the bank's windows. A line of smiling men stretched arrow-straight from the door to the teller's cage, where Crabtree and a woman teller stood shelling out money. Fargo veered right and went to the saloon. He noticed the hitching posts out front now showed several wide gaps, which meant most of last night's traffic in the saloon had sobered up and departed.

Mazie and the other two racehorses stood behind the bar, chatting with six bleary-eyed, sexually drained cow-punchers leaning on it across from them. When she spied him walk in, Mazie left the conversation and came down the bar.

Fargo said, "Now that Thurston's lost his lease, what are you and the others planning?" He nodded toward Vera and Frances.

"Odd that you would ask that. We don't know. Denver, maybe. Frances said she might try Carter's Creek."

"What's wrong with staying right here?"

"Here? In the saloon? Who would we work for?"

"Why, yourselves, of course."

"That would be up to the new owner, wouldn't it?"

"Oh, I—"

Mazie's sudden stare behind him snipped his reply and turned his head to see what had caused her brow to furrow. A shapely, petite woman, elegantly dressed, complete with a dove-gray wide brim hat with a light-brown hatband, matching wide belt, and high button shoes, stood just inside the double doors. She wore an ankle-length dress that was also dove-gray with light-brown buttons. Fargo caught the hint of a delicate perfume.

Visible behind her out front was an enclosed private coach that he presumed was hers. On the other side of the swinging doors stood a behemoth black man. He looked as though he could whip any ten men in a fair or dirty fight. He too was dressed impeccably, only in all black save the bloodred string tie. A shiny top hat sat on his clean-shaven head which glistened. The black pupils in his large eyes stared beyond Fargo and Mazie.

Mazie said, "Ma'am, this is the saloon. The hotel's acr—"

"I know," her southern drawl interrupted. "Where is the devil's son of a bitch?" All spoken without looking at Mazie or Fargo.

Fargo leaned his back on the edge of the bartop to survey the tiny woman better. Auburn tresses were gathered and tied with a light-brown bow at the back of her head. Two ringlets fell from under the hat and adorned her brow. Her face was extremely gorgeous, and the lips were full, the upper not quite as full as the lower but with high peaks that formed a Cupid's bow. His gaze lowered onto the full bosom. He imagined them unleashed. They would be firm, with precious little if any sag. She had a small waist that gave way to rounded hips.

"Which one, ma'am?" Fargo dared ask.

Eyes that matched the color of the buttons drifted onto his. After a studious pause, she considered him from head to boot and back. "Who might you be, cowboy?"

"Not a cowboy, ma'am."

"This is . . . ?" She let the question trail off. Her head turned slightly and she cut her eyes to that side. "What name is the bastard using this time?" It was obvious she spoke to the black man.

He reminded her in a soft, clear, deep baritone voice. "Douglas Thurston, Miss Vanessa."

Her eyes cut back to Fargo and Mazie.

Mazie replied, "He ain't here no more."

"Oh? Where will I find . . . Douglas?"

"Over at Doc Williamson's, ma'am," Mazie answered.

"Another heart attack?"

It sounded to Fargo that she hoped that was the case. "I suppose you could say that," he offered.

"A serious one?"

She forgot to add the "I hope" Fargo expected to hear. "Very. A bullet tore it apart."

One pretty eyebrow arched. "Then he's dead." The tone was laced with disgust.

"Yes, ma'am. Happened last night back there at the crap table."

Her head shook slowly. She came closer by two paces and sighed, "Damn. Who caught him cheating?"

"I did, ma'am. You are—"

"Vanessa Murdock, his wife . . . now his widow, I should say."

Out of respect, Fargo removed his hat. "I'm sorry, ma'am, but he was fixing to draw on me."

"I know, I know. Put your hat back on. I'm pissed because I didn't get to shoot the sorry bastard." She looked at Mazie, said, "Pour me a whiskey, darling," and stepped next to Fargo. Without looking behind her, she said, "Come on inside, Mozart."

The doors parted and the huge man stepped beside her. "Mozart Higgins," she told Fargo. "My bodyguard. My daddy gave him that name. He said his slaves needed some class. He gave Mozart to me when I left the plantation to marry that louse Claude Murdock, who will also be remembered as Antoine Devereaux, William Buckner, Charles Lamont, and now Douglas Thurston, it seems."

Fargo glanced to Mozart's huge hands palms down on the bartop, then up the powerful arms and shoulders to the man's enormous head. The hard facial features appeared as though they had been chiseled from a block of ebony granite, then buffed to shine. By way of greeting, Mozart barely nodded his head.

Fargo asked her, "Now that he's gone, what are your plans?"

Her broad shoulders shrugged. She let her gaze slide around the room, up the stairs, and back to the death scene before answering, "Run this place, I suppose." Mazie refilled their shot glasses.

The widow asked her, "What's your name, honey?"

"Mazie Freeman." She glanced up at Mozart's face. "Do you want a drink?"

He answered an octave or two above a whisper. "Bourbon, missy. In a high glass, please."

Mazie brought a bottle from under the bar and a glass from the shelf behind her.

Vanessa asked, "Do you and those other two ladies want to work for me . . . *with* me, I should say?"

Fargo instantly took a renewed interest in the new widow.

Mazie perked up. "Sure, we would, ma'am."

"Excellent. What was your split with that asshole husband of mine?"

Mazie gulped and started to answer, but Fargo spoke first. "Fifty-fifty."

Vanessa flicked questioning eyes at him and grinned, but spoke to Mazie. "Is this big fellow your manager, or your . . ." She left it hanging for one of them to finish.

"Neither," Fargo replied. "I'm their bodyguard."

Her grin widened into a smile. "I see," she said. "Well, honey, from now on you girls get to keep sixty percent. How does that sound?"

Again Mazie gulped. "Oh, ma'am, that'd be just fine with us, I'm sure."

"Should be." Vanessa snorted. "That prick wasn't giving you a penny. All you got was room and board, all the liquor you could hold, limp promises, and his hard every other day."

Just then Kid Ballas came through the doors and to the bar. "You looking for me?" he asked Fargo. Kid glanced up at the face under the top hat, flinched, and sputtered, "Gosh a'mighty, who is he?"

Vanessa looked at the kid with a sparkle in her eyes. "Come to me, you beautiful man. I want to hug you."

Kid blushed. "Aw, ma'am—"

"No, I mean it. Either you come over here or I'll—"

Mozart stepped behind Kid Ballas, lifted him from the floor, and stood him in front of Vanessa. She embraced the young cowboy, cooing, "Uhmm, you are sweet."

Fargo chuckled. "Ma'am, you can have him later. Right now he and I need to talk in private." He took Roy by an elbow, saying, "Pardon us," and led him to a table.

Roy sighed, "Doesn't she smell good?"

"Kid, they all smell good. When are you heading back to Texas?"

"I'm packed and ready to ride. Why?"

"After you report to Mr. Hollis and his wife, do you think he would let you come back to Walsenburg for a while?"

"Maybe. What for?"

Fargo tapped the Smith & Wesson. "Insurance."

Kid Ballas' face brightened. "Oh, you expecting trouble, Mr. Fargo?"

"Like I said, insurance. I expect two things to happen, both bad. One, drifters and outlaws passing through here will learn their well's gone dry. With the free handouts gone, they'll go back to robbing and killing. So far I haven't met anybody who could handle them except you. As a matter of fact, I've gone so far to have you listed as the sheriff who wants me dead or alive. The wanted poster is being printed right now.

"Two, I believe I'll be riding through the gates of hell to get the girl. Once I discover their hideout and they learn I'm not what I make out to be, it will be in their best interests to kill me."

Kid Ballas was way ahead of him. "Dang right. They'll chase you all the way here."

"All the way to Texas if need be."

"You want to make Walsenburg the branding place?"

"You got it, Kid. I'll lead the whole lot of them to town. Then you and I, that fellow Mozart over there, anybody else who wants, we'll lay them out for Doc Williamson and Reverend Orr to bury. Are you in?"

"Can't wait," Kid Ballas answered emphatically. "I'm positive Mr. Hollis will tell me to come back. He'd be the first to insist on it. I'll ride fast for Texas, even faster getting back. I wouldn't want to miss this for nothing. No, siree Bob, I wouldn't. I'll be back just as soon as I can. That's a promise, Mr. Fargo."

"Good." They stood and shook hands. "One more thing, Kid. A suggestion. Make friends with that woman. She's a few years older than you, yes, but don't let age get in the way of a good thing." Fargo shot him a wink. "While you're at it, get to know Mozart Higgins too. A man like that just might end up being the best friend you ever have."

"Yeah," Roy mused, glancing at the giant. "He'd sure make a terrible enemy, especially on a dark night."

"You could count on that being true. Kid, till we meet again, you take care." Fargo turned and touched the brim of his hat, acknowledging the widow, as he walked outside.

He went to his room at the Buckhorn. As he unlocked his door, his wild-creature hearing picked up the squeak of a plank on the top landing of the external stairs at the end of the gloomy hallway. He cut his eyes that way.

In that instant the drifter with nervous eyes fired, his shout drowned out by the roar of his gun.

5

The bullet disturbed the air, fanned the hair on the right side of Fargo's face, then thudded into the wall at the far end of the hallway. Fargo had already drawn his Colt when he turned to look at the drifter, but there was nobody to shoot. The nervous-eyed man fired the one shot, then fled.

Fargo sprinted to the door and raced down the stairs. The man was running along next to the hotel, toward the street where his horse stood loose-reined by a small water trough. He still gripped the pistol in his right hand.

Fargo took dead aim on the man's right shoulder and fired. The slug's impact knocked the dry-gulcher sideways. He stumbled over his own foot, let go of the gun, and fell facedown in the mud at the edge of the street. He tried to get up, but collapsed back down in the mud.

As Fargo hurried down the stairs, a tall husky man with two towheaded blond boys sitting next to him on the driver's seat of a California flatbed pulled up and reined to a halt. They watched Fargo come and grab the back of the downed man's shirt and pull him upright. Turning the scoundrel around to face him, Fargo had to use both hands to hold him up. "Where are the others?" Fargo growled.

The red bearded man's eyelids fluttered. Two white eyeballs—made to appear even whiter by the black mud sliding down the man's face—rolled back in the sockets. "You killed my big brother Pete." The eyelids closed and his body sagged limp.

Fargo asked the man in the wagon, "How about helping me get him to Doc Williamson?"

The man told his boys to stay put, then dropped to the ground. He took the wounded man by the armpits and

Fargo grabbed the ankles. They laid him facedown at the rear of the wagon. Fargo climbed in and held him from jostling off.

Five minutes later they reined to a halt behind a large log cabin nestled in golden aspen. "Doc's place," the man offered. "You boys wait here."

Doc Williamson's loud whiskey voice preceded his appearance at the back door to see who was trying to kick it down. "Wait a goddamn minute. I'm coming. Hell, don't tear it down."

From the sound of the voice, Fargo expected to see a bull of a man. Instead, he faced a short, frail man dressed in gray long johns and shaking a mane of unruly white hair above and surrounding a haggard face.

"Jesus Christ, Swede, not another one," Doc cried. He swung the door open.

"This one's alive, Doc," Swede said. "Where do you want him?"

"Hell, I don't know. I'm not lying all that mud on a bed, though. Put him on the kitchen table." He darted in advance of them, folded the four corners of the tablecloth to its middle, gathered in everything on it, then swung the bundle away, ordering, "Hoist him up so's I can take a look at that gunshot wound."

Fargo wiped mud off the drifter's hands and wrists while Swede cleaned the neck and face. Together they watched the doctor probe in the bloody hole with a surgical instrument to find the bullet. All three listened to the unconscious man's delirious moans. "Frank . . . I'm hit, Frank. Where are you, Russ? Gotta get to . . . they killed Pete . . . Saint Lu—"

"Aha," Doc Williamson muttered. He withdrew the slim prongs and dropped the misshapen hunk of lead in his other palm.

"How bad off is he?" Fargo asked.

"If he isn't sick, he'll be fit as a fiddle in a week's time. Friend of yours?"

"No. He's one of four drifters—outlaws who were in the saloon last night. That slug is from my gun."

Getting the dead ready for burial was one thing; the departed's relatives, if there were any, paid for Doc's services rendered, otherwise a town fund took care of his bill. Treating the sick or wounded was another matter, especially in regard to drifters. There was no fund for that. Putting salve in and around the wound, Doc asked, "Who's gonna pay my bill for keeping this fellow alive?"

Swede quickly shook his head.

Fargo said, "I will. How much?"

Doc scratched the stubble on his chin while eyeing Fargo, obviously searching for an amount the stranger could pay. "Forty dollars," he finally stated.

Fargo dug the envelope out of his hip pocket and counted off an even hundred dollars. Handing the money to the astonished doctor, he declared, "I want him on his feet and traveling by sundown today. Make him think he's not in as bad a shape as he is. Tell him he has to stay flat on his gut for another day. Then go to another room and make like you're talking to somebody. Let him hear you say they're building a hanging scaffold. He'll do the rest."

"He'll die," Doc warned. "The bullet damn near went through him. But before he does, he'll go out of his mind from fever." He looked at the money in his hand. "But if you want him up—"

"I'll bring his horse 'round back," Fargo cut in. "Let him know it's there." He looked at Swede's solemn face. "Can you drop me off at the hotel?"

Swede nodded.

Doc said, "You the same man who sent me Thurston and the others?" When Fargo nodded, Williamson said, "Come with me. I want to show you something."

They followed him into a large darkened room that was a tad chilly. Doc lit a candle. Four sheets covered as many bodies laid in a row on the floor. "Hope you men aren't squeamish," Williamson remarked. He pulled back a sheet. It was Thurston. He was naked. Doc held the candle down by Thurston's chest. Fargo's bullet had left an ugly hole slightly left of the breastbone, slightly off-center between the leering eyes of a devil's head tattooed on the chest.

"What do you make of that?" Doc Williamson asked.

"It figures," Fargo muttered.

Williamson glanced up at him. The candlelight painted Doc's face pale yellow. Fargo swore he saw a terrible fear flash up the gaunt face and collect in Doc's eyes. Doc lowered his gaze to the back of Thurston's left hand. He reached for it haltingly, as though the hand was still very much alive and might seize him. Williamson slowly turned the palm up and moved the candle flame near it. Fargo and Swede squatted and leaned in to see better. In the fleshy part between the thumb and index finger was what appeared to be a tattoo of a tiny three-petal black flower. Doc gulped and whispered, "It's the mark of the beast."

Fargo and Swede bent closer. Now they saw it wasn't a flower petal, but three sixes arranged to appear as a flower. They sat back on their haunches. Fargo asked, "What about the others?"

Doc jerked the other sheets off. Thurston's helpers, the bartender, and the man Fargo and the others had seen thrown from the porch of the saloon were stretched out nude. Williamson muttered, "Four of 'em were dirty filthy, but no tattoos." He drew the sheets up over the bodies. "I'll dress 'em later," Doc explained. "Come with me, gentlemen. I want to show you another strange thing I found." Leaving the morgue, he blew out the candle.

They followed him to his study, where he opened a desk drawer and removed a small box. He opened it and held it out for them to see inside. Fargo picked out one of the four rings, Swede another. "I took 'em off Thurston and his crowd," Doc said.

Fargo lifted out one ring which was different in one respect from the others, all of which were identical. Its devil's head was carved from fiery sapphire, while the others were from red rubies. All were set on heavy rings of silver. Holding the ring for Doc to see, Fargo said, "I'm keeping this for a while. I'll be responsible for it. Let's check the fingers on that man lying on the kitchen table." Swede dropped the ring he held to inspect back in the box.

Encircling the finger next to the little finger on the man's right hand was a ring having a ruby devil's head.

"Just as I suspected," Fargo mused. "This man wore no ring when I saw his hands at the stable yesterday evening. I think I need to have a look around Thurston's office. This many rings that look alike means something. I've seen enough. Ready to take me back, Swede?"

Swede nodded.

Doc walked them to the door. They shook his hand and left. On the way to the hotel Fargo learned that Swede was the town carpenter and that he had looked at the damage to Kaspar's livery roof. He told Kaspar he could repair it good as new for a hundred dollars.

"What did he say to that?" Fargo asked through a tight grin.

"Nothing at first. He booted a horse apple out of sight, doubled up his fists, and got all red-faced. Then he started hopping and hollered I was a robber and ought to get hemp fever."

"Is it a hundred-dollar job?"

"No. Forty or thereabouts. But the old coot's into me for sixty on other repairs he hasn't paid."

Fargo counted out sixty dollars and handed it to him. "Go back and make him think you have a change in heart. I owe that old man, but don't let him know I squared his account with you."

Swede reined to a halt in front of the Buckhorn. Fargo tousled the boys' straw-colored hair, shot both winks, and dropped to the ground.

Ben Voss watched from the porch. He said, "Mr. Fargo, this is fast becoming a nice town to live in again. Is that man you shot dead?"

"No, he's still breathing. But only barely. Coming down the stairs, I noticed three horses under the shed out back. Yours?"

"Sure are. You need one?"

"What I need is for you to trail one to Doc Williamson's. I'll ride the drifter's."

Voss flinched. "You mean you're going to take his horse to him? After what he tried to do to you?"

Fargo chuckled.

Fifteen minutes later they were putting Voss's two horses back under the shed. Walking back to the porch,

Fargo cautioned, "Shortly before sundown that man's horse will come charging up the street with him leaning low in the saddle. I'd appreciate it if you'd help spread the word for nobody to shoot him. And I'd be obliged if after you see him rush past, you'd come wake me up. Knock once, count to four, and knock again. That way I won't shoot you."

Voss's Adam's apple bobbed as he gulped and nodded.

Fargo went to the saloon. Mazie told him Vanessa and her towering bodyguard were in Thurston's office behind the alcove. When he entered, Vanessa was seated behind Thurston's big desk with her ankles crossed on its top. Mozart sat in one of the plush red chairs. A grandfather clock Fargo hadn't noticed before stood crosswise in the corner to the right of the desk. It chimed the half-hour.

"Yes, Mr. Fargo, what can I help you with?" She smiled.

"I'm looking for rings. Have you found any?"

"No, but then I haven't yet started searching through his stuff." She lowered her feet to the floor and stood. "Help yourself, Mr. Fargo." She came around the desk and sat in the other chair.

Fargo started opening desk drawers. The lower right and left were the same size, only the right was half as deep. Fargo put the stuff in it on top of the desk, then used his Arkansas toothpick to play around the edges of what he suspected was a false bottom. The tip triggered a spring. The bottom raised on the near end. Inside the secret compartment he found a shallow box made from rosewood. He set it on the desktop and opened the lid. The inside was covered with black felt with narrow indented slots, with nothing in twenty-three of them. Standing in the other twenty-seven slots were rings identical to the one worn by the wounded drifter. "What was your departed husband's fascination with Satan?"

"He never really said, although I did ask. All I ever got him to say was, 'Darling, one day the devil will make us rich.' To this day I don't know what possessed me to marry the bastard. It certainly wasn't his prowess in the bed. By any name he never satisfied me."

"Then why did you marry him?"

"I really can't say for certain. Perhaps it was his lifestyle that drew me to him. Hell, I was young, easily impressed. He was good-looking, suave. Little did I realize I would end up working in saloons, being his bright eyes in poker games . . . and doing other things, naughty things, for him. It got so I found escape from the reality through those naughty things."

She chuckled before continuing. "Escape? He's the one who escaped. Left me lying high and wet in a New Orleans saloon bed. I ended up owning the place. Earlier this year I sold the saloon. I added the money to my savings, which alone was a handsome amount, and started tracking him down. I wanted to kill him. For what he did to me, the way he used me, and to others. What do you think was his fascination for the devil?"

"Ever hear him mention a Saint Lucifer?"

"Yes. He mentioned it once. Lucifer I understood, what with that horrible tattoo and all. I asked what the Saint meant. He said Lucifer was God's favorite angel, so he had to be a saint. The man had a warped mind, Mr. Fargo. Why do you ask about Saint Lucifer?"

"Drifters, outlaws, were overheard mentioning it. They referred to it as a place."

"I wouldn't know its location. Would you, Mozart?"

"Not exactly, Miss Vanessa."

Fargo's eyes kicked on to Mozart's. "Then roughly," Fargo said.

"I heard Mr. Murdock tell a man his Saint Lucifer would be in the exact opposite place of Hades. The man asked him to explain that. Mr. Murdock told him, 'Below slum-something.' I didn't catch the last part of it because somebody in the saloon laughed real loud."

"But you did hear 'below slum'?"

"Yes, sir."

"Both of you have been a big help. If there's anything I can ever do to—"

"Chase that delicious cowboy over here to me," Vanessa hastened to interrupt. She had that sparkle in her eyes again.

Fargo touched the brim of his hat and left. He went to his room at the hotel and lay down to have a nap. He dozed off with two thoughts in mind: that the drifter would live long enough to lead him to Saint Lucifer, and the place wouldn't be the hell he imagined.

His internal alarm roused him awake at two o'clock. He dressed and walked to the Schuttes' place of business. Malva greeted him with a big smile. "Your rush order is coming off the press. Come in and see for yourself."

Fargo followed her to where John worked at a press. It looked to Fargo as though most of the black ink was on her husband; smudges on his nose and one cheek dominated those on his hands and apron. As they watched, John pulled a heavy cylinder over a brown sheet of paper.

Malva explained, "We're using brown paper because it's more sinister-looking. I thought sinister is what you wanted."

John peeled the paper off the wood etching and type and held it for Fargo to see. "Remarkable," Fargo told them. "You did a perfect job on the eyes. 'Skye Fargo. Wanted dead or alive.' That should do it. How much do I owe you?"

"Altogether . . . What, John? Ten for the drawing . . ."

"Oh, twenty-five will be enough, you cleaning up the town and all," John replied.

Fargo gave him forty. "All I did was get rid of some stinking garbage. Thanks anyhow."

John handed the poster to his customer. Fargo bid them good day and left. He went next door to the jail and stuck the poster on a rusty nail driven into the front wall by the dirty window. He backed to the edge of the porch, drew the Colt, and shot holes in the zeros of the dollar amount.

Back in his hotel room he folded the bullet-riddled poster and put it in his saddlebags. Then he headed for the café.

Vanessa and Mozart were seated across from each other at one of the tables next to the windows. Neither had food or drink before them. Millie stood talking with Vanessa. Fargo caught the tail end of it. ". . . glad to do that in the saloon, Mrs. Murdock." She looked up when Fargo crossed to take a counter stool.

The widow said, "Mr. Fargo, please join us. We haven't ordered yet."

Fargo moved to the chair beside her.

"I have pot roast and all the trimmings today," Millie advised.

All three heads nodded. Each asked for coffee while waiting.

Fargo noticed Vanessa kept glancing toward the saloon. "Figuring out what to do?" he asked.

Millie arrived with the coffee.

Mozart nodded.

She answered after sighing heavily. "Yes. That saloon is the filthiest place I've ever seen. The smell is horrible, isn't it, Mozart?"

He nodded; she went on. "I'm closing it down until it's scrubbed clean, painted inside and out, and my new sign is up. Claude never did know how to do things right." They sipped from their coffees before Vanessa continued. "Mozart, find the town carpenter. I want him to build quarters for you and an apartment for me adjacent to the back of the place."

Millie set platters of steaming food on the table.

As they filled their plates, Mozart said, "I heard you shot a man."

"After he shot at me. A drifter. Mad because I killed his brother last night. He'll be okay."

The widow studied Fargo's chiseled face while she chewed a mouthful of carrots and potatoes. She swallowed, chased it with a sip of coffee, and asked, "Doesn't this town have a sheriff?"

"No, ma'am. Your husband had him and the deputy shot first thing."

"The sorry bastard. Well, Mr. Fargo, if the town won't, I'll pay you to be the new sheriff. One hundred a month plus all the bourbon you can hold and you know what. How does that sound?"

"Mighty generous. Can't do it, though. I have other business to tend to."

"Saint Lucifer?"

"Yes. Try making that offer to Kid Ballas when he gets back from Texas."

Her face seemed to blossom younger, prettier, and a darling twinkle appeared in her eyes. "That lovable young man I hugged earlier? Really, Mr. Fargo, why he's too sweet and inno—"

Fargo and Mozart burst out laughing. It was Mozart who explained, "Miss Vanessa, that kid, he's no boy. That kid's a mean son of a bitch if he has to be. Isn't that right?"

"Deadlier than a rattler, ma'am," Fargo agreed. "That Smith and Wesson he totes low makes him big as six full-grown men. Kid Ballas is the type who smiles as he sends you through hell's front gate. But you're right about one thing: he is innocent."

She blinked at the revelation, but said nothing.

Fargo finished his meal, excused himself, and stood. "Swede Torger is the carpenter, ma'am. He's a good family man, strong as a bull. I'll be leaving about sunset and won't be back for a while. You two take care. I'll see you when I return." He touched the brim of his hat and left.

Passing through the hotel lobby, he reminded Ben Voss to awaken him when the time came. Fargo stretched out on the bed to catch more sleep while he waited. He knew he'd be in the saddle all night and wanted to be completely rested and alert.

The knock shot his eyes open. Four heartbeats and the second knock came. "I'm up," Fargo told him. "Thank you. I'll be right down."

Both of the Vosses were at the foot of the stairs when Fargo, saddlebags over his shoulder and gripping the Sharps, came down them. "Pounded west just like you said he would," Ben said. "Leaning, almost touching the horse's neck. Shirttail out, flying in the wind."

"Fine. I'll let him get a good head start, think he got away clean. How much is my bill?"

"One doll—"

Ben cut his financially minded spouse off with a quick wave of the hand. "Nothing," he blurted.

Fargo glanced at the sheepish expression on Freida's face. Crossing the lobby, he dropped a silver dollar on the registration counter. "See you again," he said, going through the door.

At the livery he settled up with Neil Kaspar and made the Ovaro ready for the trail. The old man followed him to the entrance, where he bade Fargo good luck and good hunting.

Fargo rode west and quickly picked up the drifter's tracks. The full moon made it possible to tell from the spacing of the hoofprints that the man had his horse in a gallop.

About four in the morning he rounded a sharp bend and met a man and woman in a buckboard. Fargo reined the pinto to a halt next to the wagon and said, "Mister, you can lower that rifle. I'm a peaceable man, but the one ahead of me isn't. Did he say anything when he passed?"

"No," she answered. "I don't think he even saw us."

"He looked hurt," the gaunt man beside her added. "All but lying on the horse's neck. You after him?"

"Sure am. How far to Carter's Creek?"

"You're nearly there. Alma and me, we're on our way to Walsenburg for supplies. Hope you catch him before he falls off."

Fargo nodded, told them thanks, and spurred the pinto forward.

Dawn broke. Four white-tail doe sauntered across the trail in front of him, then the buck. Birds stirred in the aspens on both sides of him. Nature was in the process of going to bed or waking up. An unseen creek gurgled off to Fargo's left and an owl hooted good night. Fargo's man was nowhere in sight. But Carter's Creek loomed straight ahead, its few structures still bathed in heavy shadows of early morning. Most of the cabins dotting the slopes had light shining through at least one window. Only a spotted dog noticed Fargo ride through the hamlet. It trotted alongside the Ovaro, wagging its tail. Panting easily, the dog seemed to be smiling. It followed for a distance before turning back.

The sun was well up, its warm rays feeling good on Fargo's back, when he saw the drifter's tracks angle off the trail and enter a rush of blue spruce. Fargo knew the man was tired beyond belief and hurt like hell. He was calling it quits for a while. He needed rest, a few hours' sleep to help regain his strength.

Fargo rode about a mile farther, then he too left the trail and went high to a cluster of boulders surrounded by golden aspen. Then he dismounted and sat to wait.

The sun had lowered behind the mountain peaks. The trail was now cast in light shadows. Munching on beef jerky, Fargo heard the drifter coming before he saw him. He had the horse in a walk and no longer rode leaning forward. Fargo watched him till he disappeared, then mounted up.

Fargo knew this trail led to Alamosa and beyond. At the drifter's pace Alamosa was still a day-and-a-half ride away. He stopped and slept when the drifter did, which was often. The man was obviously weakening. Fargo wondered if the man would make it to Alamosa, but the fellow did.

He entered the little town shortly before midnight of the third day. Fargo watched him slide from the saddle and loose-rein his horse in front of the saloon. The Trailsman reined the Ovaro around behind a building across the street from the saloon and sat easy in the saddle to watch and wait.

He didn't have to wait long. The drifter and another man came outside and went to one end of the saloon. The drifter shoved him around the corner of the building. After a few minutes the drifter emerged counting money. He went back in the saloon and had two drinks while talking to the bartender, who was pointing, obviously giving directions. The man came out and got on his horse. Fargo followed him to a house. The man shouted to awaken the occupants. A lamp was lit. It moved through the house to the front door. A man dressed for bed opened the door and looked out. They spoke, then both went inside. A half-hour passed before Fargo's quarry came back out and saddled up. He rode toward the main trail. When he was out of sight, Fargo went and knocked on the door.

"Yes, what is it?" an angry voice bellowed. The lamp's glow moved back toward the door. "I'm coming, I'm coming."

The door opened. Fargo immediately detected the unmistakable odor of alcohol, not on the man's breath, but in the house. "Are you a doctor?" Fargo inquired.

"Not another one," the man whined. "Come on in and I'll look at it."

"No need," Fargo replied. "I shot the man who was just here. I'm tracking him. Did he by any chance mention where he was headed?"

"No. Said he hated to wake me, but he needed tending to. Didn't say nothing else."

"How bad is he? Doc Williamson over in Walsen—"

"I know Doc," he cut in. "The man's in bad shape. I advised him to take it easy for a few days and come back tomorrow. He's already got a fever."

"Is there a slum something or other near here?"

"Slum? No, not that I know of."

"How about a place called Saint Lucifer?"

The doctor looked at him quizzically for a second or two, started to say something, but shut the door instead. Fargo heard him pad away barefoot, mumbling to himself.

The drifter had headed back toward the main trail. As Fargo neared town, he saw several men hurrying across the street. At the corner of the intersection, he turned west and saw the men looking through the window of a business. He paused when he came to them and asked, "What's going on?" He noticed the window had been broken out. The sign above the door read NEW AND USED FIREARMS.

A man answered, "Somebody just busted into Duke Moncrief's place."

Fargo rode on, knowing the drifter was now armed. The wounded man's tracks left the trail about five miles west of Alamosa. Fargo continued a distance and angled right. He spread the bedroll among trees on a knoll, then lay down and went to sleep.

A horse's whinny flicked his eyes open. Dawn had broken. The sky was clear. He sat and watched the drifter ride by, now carrying a six-gun. Fargo waited till he was out of sight, then mounted up and followed.

After sunset they cleared a village named Del Norte. Shortly thereafter the drifter stopped for the night. Fargo proceeded to a trapper's trading post where the westward trail was joined by another from the southwest. He stopped short of the post and moved to high ground that overlooked the junction. He spread the bedroll and got some shut-eye.

The faint sounds of conversation carried in the morning breeze whipped Fargo's eyes open. He stood and looked down on the log cabin's sod roof. In front of it stood the drifter's mount. Two men and a beefy, broad-hipped woman wearing a beat-up cowboy hat were laughing.

Fargo left the Ovaro to graze while he crept down to hear better. With his ear plastered to the back of the trading post he heard the drifter saying, ". . . so I guess Russell will be running things now."

The trapper answered, "Tell him he can count on me. By the way, Howie, tell Russ a small wagon train came by a few days ago, heading for Creede, I think. Anyhow, there was two good-looking women on it—the kind he likes. Tell him I said so."

Fargo had heard enough. The trapper and his woman were an outpost—eyes and ears for Saint Lucifer, which had to be close, somewhere near Creede. Fargo eased back up the slope, walked the pinto through the trees till he was out of sight of the cabin, then mounted and headed for Creede at a gallop.

He entered Creede at sunset and went straight to the livery. He chatted with the stable boy while cleaning the pinto's hooves. "Boy, you ever heard of slum something?"

"No, sir. I'm new here. All I've heard is work harder and work faster. That sure is a nice horse you have. Wish he was mine."

"Well, maybe one day you'll have one. That saloon I passed. Do they have a—"

The boy grimaced and looked down. Reluctantly, he mumbled, "Yes, sir, they have a whore. Her name's Buttercup."

Fargo looked at the twelve-year-old freckled-faced boy and blinked. "Give him plenty of good oats and hay, all the water he wants." He draped his saddlebags over a shoulder, picked up the Sharps, and headed for the saloon.

The saloon was single-level, constructed with pine logs, built low, and not very big. Fargo had to dip his head to clear the top of the door. The bar had standing room for about six customers. A slim bartender with muttonchop sideburns and a big mustache stood talking with two men holding beers. Two small tables were against the opposite wall. In one of the chairs sat a freckled-face redhead who reminded Fargo of a whore by the name of Nadine he'd bedded in Utah. This one held a glass half-filled with amber liquid. This one also had slightly larger breasts. She stared at Fargo as though he was meat on the table. He came over and sat across from her. "Buttercup, I need to stretch out for a while. You any good at working soreness out of a tired man's butt?"

She handed him the glass. Through buck teeth separated by a perfect spitting gap, she replied, "Don't know about that working soreness out. Most claim I put soreness in. How'd you know my name?"

"The tooth fairy told me."

"Tooth fairy my ass. Rayford, he told you."

"Who's Rayford?"

"That kid brother of mine at the livery, that's who."

"How about getting us a fresh bottle and taking it to your room?"

"Be glad to. It's out back. Go on, you'll see it. I'll get the bottle."

He pushed through the rear door of the saloon and went to a one-room log cabin fifteen paces behind it. A pillowcase covered the one window. A porcelain bowl filled with water sat on the floor beneath it. The iron-barred headboard of the bed was jammed against the wall opposite the door. There was no chair or bureau, no mirror or pictures on the walls. Several folded towels set by the washbowl.

Fargo stood the Sharps in a corner and dropped the saddlebags by the stock. The Colt went under the pillow and the gun belt on the floor next to the bed. He started undressing.

Buttercup entered with the bottle in one hand and a smile on her face. She pitched the bottle on the bed and came to him, licking her lips. Raising her slender body up on tiptoes, she curled a slim arm around his neck and drew his lips to hers. They kissed openmouthed as he cupped a breast in one hand and fondled her buttocks with the other.

Buttercup moaned, "Oh, oh, oh . . . damn, you taste so good. Uhmm, yes." Her free hand went to his crotch and squeezed. Her eyes flared and her breathing quickened. She murmured, "Oh, yes, big man . . . oh, yes." Her hot tongue probed with renewed interest, eager anticipation.

He slipped the shoulders straps of her white cotton dress off. Still savoring the moist kiss, she wiggled to make it fall around her feet. He slipped the hand around and stroked her dampness. She gasped, "Yes, yes . . . don't stop." He cupped first one breast then the other and applied pressure. She squirmed, mewing, "Oh, me, where did you come from . . . where have you been? Take me, please take me."

Her fingers started working his buttons free. She broke the kiss to pull his shirt off, then gasped when she saw and felt his pectoral muscles. "God, you have a beautiful body," she whispered. The fingers darted to his fly and undid those buttons. She reached in and massaged him with both hands, gasped, "Oh, Jesus, I want this."

He picked her up and laid her on the bed, then sat on its edge to pull off his boots, Levi's, and undergarments. As he did, she closed her eyes, rubbed his hard back, and writhed. He half-turned and let his gaze roam over her slim body. The breasts were half again the size of champagne glasses, the large areolae light brown with a dash of soft red, the nipples generous and youthful pinkish brown. Tiny freckles were everywhere on her milk-white skin. They continued over her flat belly and smallish, indented navel to disappear in her bush of flaming-red pubic hair. He bent to nibble first one then the other nipple till they stood erect and hard. She sucked in a series of quick breaths, uttering, "Oh, God! Oh, God! I feel that . . . to my toes! Bite them! Oh, yes . . . bite! Please bite!"

Fargo sucked in most all of a firm breast, coursed his tongue around the areola, then bit gently. She shrieked, "Oh, goddamn! I'm on fire! Oh, that's so wonderful! The other one. Get it too, big man. Please."

As he shifted to the other supple breast, her hands gripped his stiff manhood. As she stroked him, she arched her back. She squirmed her chest to thrust the breast hard into his mouth and whimpered, "I'm ready . . . give it to me . . . I want all of it. Yes, yes, all of it."

He rolled her onto her stomach and lifted her by the waist. Gasping, she drew her knees up and spread them, buried her face in the pillow, and grabbed hold of iron bars. "Oh, God, take me, take me now. Hurry, big man."

Her body was trembling under his grip on her hips. He looked down at the swollen lower lips visible through the glistening hair, and positioned the crown of his throbbing member to penetrate them. He parted the lips with his red summit. She gasped, "Oh, God!" He hunched forward and both felt the initial entry. She gulped. "All the way. Please."

She pushed, he shoved. "Aaaayeeeiii," she screamed, and her knuckles turned white from her hard grip on the bars. He went deeper, and she screamed again, then whimpered, "Oh, oh, that's so filling, so nice . . . oh, yes."

The bed squeaked and groaned from their hard thrusts and shoves, their wild hip movements, the rolling and gyrating. Her heels came up and dug into his hard buttock cheeks, encouraging him to go deeper and faster. She got a fresh grip on the bars, pushed till her arms were straight, writhed to part her buttocks wider so he could power in more easily and harder. She screamed continuously now, "Yes!" and hollered, "Faster, please go faster . . . harder, big man!"

Her contractions felt as though a giant hand had seized him. They squeezed, wrenched, relaxed, and started all over. His mighty explosion triggered four of her own. With each, she gasped, "Oh, God!" With the last aftertremor, which milked the last drop from him, she cried, "So hot, so hot!" She shuddered. The heels fell away. Her hands slid down the bars. He felt her body sag under his firm grip. "I'm in heaven," she sighed joyously. "It's beautiful."

Fargo released her and lay by her. He rolled her onto

his muscled body and nestled her head in the crook of his shoulder. Their bodies were wringing wet with sweat, and both breathed hard. He rubbed her ass and back while her finger drew little circles on his chest. Slowly they became calm and relaxed.

She spoke first. "Did you come to stay or are you just passing through?"

"Passing. But I'll be back."

"When?"

"Hard to say. Soon, if I'm lucky."

"Trapping or gold?"

"Neither, although trapping is closest."

"Oh? Nobody comes way the hell out here unless it's to trap or hunt for gold."

"Then why are you out here?"

"No, no, I meant men. I'm doing this because it's all I know how to do. I'm a poor housekeeper and I hate milking cows."

"Huh," Fargo snorted. "You sure as hell know how to milk a man."

"Yeah, that was pretty good, wasn't it, big man?"

"Cream rose to the top."

"Well, I had a lot to work with. You didn't answer my nosy question."

"I'm chasing a man who's behind me."

Her head raised. She rolled her pale-green eyes back. "Mister, I know I'm dumb, so you'll have to explain that one to me."

"I know he's coming here, so I got out in front of him. That's where you come in."

"Me? Now I know you better explain."

"I need a spy. Will a hundred dollars buy me one? You?"

"Mister, if this town had a mayor, I'd shoot him for a hundred dollars. Less than that. What do you want me to do?"

"His name is Howie. I don't know his last name. But you'll damn sure recognize him when you see him. One, he's wounded in the right shoulder, on the back. I shot him after he shot at me and ran. Two, he's wearing a ring on his right third finger. A red ruby carved into a devil's head."

"You're kidding me."

"No, I'm not. Third, his eyes can't stay still. They keep sliding off you. He'll come for a drink or two. He smells to high heaven but—"

"I lay with stinking men all the time," she interrupted. "It goes with the business."

He nodded and continued. "Honey up to him. See if you can get him to talk. I want to know where he's going and how much longer it will take him to get there. He might ask if you want to go with him. If he does, he'll make all sorts of big promises. Maybe that's how you can learn where he's going. Tell him that you can't go right now but that you will come to him in a day or two. Believe me, you don't want to go anywhere with this man, not even to a bed. Incidentally, I'll be sleeping in this one, so you're out of business till I leave. I'll make it worth your while. He will ride west. When he does, come wake me."

"You don't want him to know you're here."

"Absolutely not. You ever hear of slum something?"

" 'Fraid not. But I'll ask around without mentioning why."

"Good. Now, get out of here or I'll never get any sleep."

"Aw, once more before I leave?"

"No, Buttercup. Between the Ovaro and you I'm all tuckered."

"Who's she?"

"She's a magnificent black-and-white stallion." He rolled her off him.

She kissed his nipples, stood, and slipped on her dress. At the door she shot him a wink before stepping outside.

Fargo stretched out and went to sleep.

The door opening snapped his eyes open. The dark form of a man stood in the doorway. He held a six-gun aimed at Fargo's head. The drifter's voice said, "I won't miss this time."

6

The Colt fired first. The man catapulted out of the doorway, jerking the trigger. The bullet whined in the night. Fargo rose and went to the door. Blood covered the front of the man's chest. His unseeing eyes stared at the full moon. Buttercup lay crumpled just outside the back door to the saloon.

The bartender eased around one side of the saloon, a man wearing a heavy coat around the other. Both were armed with pistols.

"Get her inside," Fargo barked. "I don't feel any blood on her. I'll be in soon as I pull on some clothes."

He laid her in the bartender's outstretched arms. The other fellow opened the back door. Fargo checked the Big Dipper, noted the hour was about two in the morning, and went back inside the cabin and dressed hurriedly. Within minutes he entered the dimly lit saloon. Buttercup lay faceup on the bar. Her chest rose and fell in a slow, even rhythm.

The bartender said, "Name's Al, mister. Like you said, she's okay. He knocked her out. There's a goose egg on the back of her head."

"Yeah, mine's Fargo. What went on in here? Before this, I mean?"

In the light, Fargo saw the other man wore a sheepskin coat. He was on the shorter side but stockily built and had a wild black beard, mustache, bushy eyebrows, and a mane of hair that matched. His was a prospector's clothes and hat. Fargo reckoned him to be no older than himself. The man said, "We was out front at the time, so we don't know. They was sitting at that table over there, her on his lap and then we went out for fresh air."

"Chill's right, mister. Next thing we heard was those two shots out back."

"He went one way and me the other," Chill replied.

Fargo slapped her face gently. "Get a wet rag. She's down kind of deep."

Al wiped her face with the rag, then her neck and shoulders. After a few seconds her eyes fluttered open. "Where am I?" she moaned.

"Take it easy, honey," Fargo said in a soothing voice. "Bring us in focus, then you can sit up."

Buttercup blinked a few times, shook the fuzzies from her brain, and raised to sit with their help. She looked at Fargo. "I told you I'm dumb. Where'd he go?"

"I shot him to hell. What happened in here?"

"Give me a whiskey, somebody." Al started pouring four drinks. She went on. "Like you said, he drifted in shortly after one o'clock. Chill came in a little later. I knew by them eyes it was him—the drifter, I mean. To make sure, I put my arm over his right shoulder. He dipped it and told me it was sore 'cause he fell on it.

"Said he didn't have the money to buy me a drink, so I bought his. We got to talking. You know—where you been, where you going, and that kind of stuff. He didn't ask if I wanted to go with him, so I asked if he'd get me out of here. I told him I'd be eternally grateful and all that. He wouldn't say where he'd been or where he was going. He said he needed to catch a few hours' sleep, then be on his way. I asked if he was trapping or hunting gold. He just snickered.

"When Al and Chill went outside, he asked where my room was. That's when I got dumb. I told him out back, but somebody was using it. Next thing I knew, he dumped me on the floor and headed for the back door. I ran and caught up with him just as he was opening it. I tried to pull him back. He got right in my ear and growled, 'Sister, I know who's in your bed. I saw his horse in a stall in Walsenburg, same one in the livery here.' He pulled his gun. I tried to yell, but couldn't. He yanked me outside, closed the door, and busted me one on the head."

"What did you find out about slum?" Fargo asked.

"Noth—"

Chill broke in. "Slumgullion? What about it?"

Fargo's eyes moved onto Chill's. "You know the place? Where it is, how to get there?"

"Yes. I've been through Slumgullion Pass a couple of times. Prospecting. Didn't find any gold, though."

"How do I get there?"

"Santa María Lake's 'bout three hours ride southwest of here. When you see the lake, head northwest till you come to a creek. That'll be Spring Creek. It's in a valley. Follow the valley north. It'll put you at the foot of high country. Hell, you'll see those big old mountains from miles away. It's a hard climb, mister, but you'll find Spring Creek Pass. That's just the beginning. Keep going and you'll come to Slumgullion Pass. It's a helluva lot higher than Spring Creek Pass. It's treacherous up there, what with landslides and all this time of the year, so keep your eyes and ears open for falling rocks."

"All right. What's below Slumgullion Pass?"

The unruly beard and mustache spread and revealed Chill's smile. There was a faraway twinkle in his eyes. "Some of the most gorgeous high country you'll ever see. At the bottom is Lake San Cristobal on the Little Fork River. Prettiest sight you'll ever see. Might say, heaven on earth."

"You been there recently—say, within the last six months?"

"No. Last time I crossed the pass was last summer."

"Anybody there? Down around the river or lake, that is?"

"Not a soul. Mister, that's mighty rough country. Take my advice and have a couple of pack mules with you."

"I think I can handle it. One more thing." Fargo looked at Al. "Any women disappear from around here in the last six months?"

Al shook his head.

Buttercup said, "Not from here, but one on a wagon train got lost west of here."

"Lost?" Chill asked, surprised.

"According to Rayford. He talked to her husband when he came looking for her. She went behind the bushes to relieve herself and never came back."

Fargo asked Chill, "Where does the Little Fork go?"

"I think it's the Tomichi. 'Bout two days north of Lake San Cristobal. Pretty country. Like I said, no gold, though."

Fargo downed his drink. To Buttercup he said, "Let's go back to bed."

She hopped off the bartop, cut him a naughty smile, and led the way. She was undressed and up on her hands and knees on the bed by the time he cleared the door. He pulled his clothes off and lay down beside her. "Honey, this time I'll show you how the Navajos romp." He pulled her atop him. Half an hour later they were both exhausted. Sleep came easy and fast.

Two roosters crowing popped Fargo's eyes open at daybreak. He yawned, stretched, and looked at Buttercup lying half on and half off him with one arm laid across his chest. He nudged her awake.

" 'Morning, big feller," she whispered drowsily.

"Hated to wake you, honey, but I have to be on my way. Any food around here this time of day?"

"You wait here in bed. I'll run over to Ma Coombs' and fix something for us. Ma's always up first thing. I eat with her all the time. She won't mind." She slipped out of bed and dressed.

Fargo watched her leave, then turned over and went back to sleep. Half an hour later she came back carrying two plates of food. Ma was behind her with a coffeepot, cups, and utensils.

"Buttercup said you was big," Ma began, her voice cracky with advanced age. "She didn't say whopping big or I'd've cooked two more eggs."

Fargo sat and used the pillow as a table. The two women sat on the floor. Buttercup ate and Ma sipped coffee. Both watched him like a pair of starved buzzards.

Ma said, "Buttercup told me that man you shot had on a devil's ring." He nodded. Ma volunteered, "I seen one before."

Fargo swallowed a bite of ham and eggs. "Where?"

"Right here in Creede. Seth Magee had it on."

"Who might he be?"

"Trapper-trader. His place is back down the trail a ways."

"I saw it. A sod-roof trading post where a trail south meets this one."

"That's it. Seth and his donkeys went through here about three months back. He stopped to water his animals out front of Slocum's place. I was delivering eggs to Slocum at the time. That red ring caught my fancy . . . till I saw what it was. I told Seth he ought to throw that damn thing away. Humph, he told me to mind my own business."

"When he left, he went toward the lake?"

"Sure did."

Fargo ate a biscuit first. "I know others wearing rings like it have been through here. I believe all of them would have stopped at the saloon. Buttercup's new to town. She didn't know about them till I told her. But there should have been two other men pass through here in the last two days. Think back, Buttercup, you too, Mrs. Coombs . . . Are you sure you didn't see a ring on one of them? Also, Mrs. Coombs, about two months ago two men and a blond girl should have rode through. Did you see them?"

Both females shook their heads.

Ma said, "Buttercup said you was going to Slumgullion."

"That's right." He held his empty cup out for her to refill.

"I been there once, long time ago. Charlie, he's my departed, he didn't come this way to get there. There's another route north of the trail to Walsenburg. Rough as all hell, but shorter as the crow flies. No towns or nothing. You gotta know what you're doing to be back in there. Maybe those other men went that way."

Fargo put his empty plate aside. "Maybe so. Do you know the Little Fork?"

"I've been on it. Why?"

"I have reason to believe those men with devil's-head rings have been stealing women. Where would they get them?"

"The only place they could is off wagon trains on the trail between Pueblo and Grand Junction. Part of it follows the Tomichi. Little Fork runs into the Tomichi. Long ride from Slumgullion, though. You want me to fix you some more eggs? I have plenty."

"No, I'm full, thank you. Although I haven't ridden it in quite a while, I know that trail. You ladies have been a big help. I won't forget it. Now, how about stepping outside while I get dressed?" He handed Ma his empty cup.

"I seen men naked before," she said.

Fargo noted a hint of wistfulness in her tone and longing in her eyes. He threw the sheet back and sat on the edge of the bed to dress.

"Buttercup, I'd give everything I ever owned to be your age again and have this man in my bed. Mister, yours is the most beautiful body I ever saw. Uh, huh."

Fargo shot her a wink and put his hat on. Ten minutes later he was making the Ovaro ready to ride.

Rayford said, "That man you shot in the heart last night, he was in here after you. He admired your horse, asked where you was."

"You told him?"

"After he said he wanted to make you an offer. I told him to go check with Buttercup."

"Learn to keep your mouth shut, boy. The words 'I don't know' usually end most questions. Buttercup got a bad headache, the man got killed, and I lost a lot of sleep."

Rayford followed him as far as the entrance. After Fargo was in the saddle, the boy said, "Mister, take me with you. I hate this place."

Fargo studied the lad's pleading face a few seconds. "Don't be hard on your big sister. People have to survive best as they know how. I can't take you with me, boy. I'm riding straight into hell." He spurred the pinto to a walk.

A short time later he topped a rise and reined the Ovaro to a halt. Before him was placid Santa María Lake, its surface mirroring the lake-blue sky and Fargo's eyes. After viewing the tranquil scene a moment, he angled the stallion to head northwest.

Fargo followed alongside the creek that fed the lake. The creek meandered a distance, then turned more north to south on the broad valley floor. Lovely mountains framed the pregnant valley on both sides and at the northern end far in the distance.

The mountains were covered with forests. Depending on terrain contour and angle of sun, Fargo saw all the shades, tints, and hues in forests of blue spruce interrupting the otherwise monotonous dark greens of tall, sedate conifers. Quaking groves of aspen streaked down the sunlit slopes, their brilliant reds, yellows, and golds adding even more color to the majestic panorama. A pair of yellow-bellied sapsuckers flew across his path.

The Ovaro walked through a blaze of color. Ferns and wildflowers grew here in profusion. Intermingled were the deep blues of mountain gentian, golden yellows of false lupine, white clusters of pearly everlasting.

Sunflowers twisted on tall sticky stems to follow and tilt their sparkling yellow and deep-brown-red faces to the sun. Patches of rosy-pink fireweed and brilliant red Indian paintbrush dotted the landscape.

The mixture of colors blended as it swept to the bases of the mountains, creating yet another unique natural color. The delicate scents and aromas filled the valley.

Fargo paused at noon to let the Ovaro graze while he reclined near the creek's bank to rest and munch on beef jerky. White puffy clouds, some with dark-gray bottoms, floated lazily over the western crests. He looked to the far end of the valley. Those crests towered high. From the looks of things he knew the paths up them would be steep.

In midafternoon he reached the base of the mountain he had selected for his ascent. During the slow approach he considered several upward routes and chose one. He began climbing. The ground conditions were excellent, affording the pinto good footing. The fresh, clean scent of pine permeated the mountain forest. He halted occasionally to dismount and rest the Ovaro while he checked its hooves and shoes for good condition and security. The last thing Fargo needed in high country was a lame horse.

Here tall high country ponderosa pine dominated the other conifers and stands of aspen. In the canopy birds nested and flourished in abundance. Nearby, a woodpecker in search of a worm hammered on a dead tree. Through the shafts of sunlight penetrating the canopy flitted tiny house wrens. Out of curiosity tree swallows swooped to light on lower branches, cocked their heads to study the intruder, then, satisfied, flew away. Red crowned yellow-bellied sapsuckers like the pair he'd seen earlier in the valley also came to check out what had entered this part of the mountain forest.

Fargo looked down on the valley. From this lofty height the valley, for as far as he could see down its length and across its width, was painted in a rainbow of dazzling colors. A patch of the rosy-pink fireweed caught his eye. A soft smile betrayed his thought. It reminded him of Kid Ballas' blush when the widow embraced him.

He returned to the saddle and continued the upward climb. Spring Creek Pass was his immediate destination. He would find it in the thin air at an altitude of nearly eleven thousand feet, where the erratic line formed by nature—the Continental Divide—crossed through it.

As he rode, he noticed signs of nature's larger animals that moved to high country during the summer. Passing through a stand of quaking aspen, he saw vertical scratches on several tree trunks, telltale marks of bear and bobcat having used them to sharpen their flesh-ripping claws. On others were tooth marks left by elk and deer. To the untrained eye they would be mistaken for initials of someone who had paused to carve them in the whitish bark between the warty scars.

There was virtually no transition from daylight to dark. When the sun lowered behind the western ranges, night swiftly followed and halted him still short of the pass. The thin air, comfortable when the sun was out, suddenly became cold.

Fargo unsaddled the pinto and spread his bedroll on smooth ground in an outcrop of large rocks surrounded by pine. On the flat-top surface of one of the gray-white stones flecked with webs of black he built a small cooking fire and brewed a pot of coffee. He drank it to knock off the chill and to wash down his trail meal of beans and beef jerky. After eating, he removed his gun belt, boots, and hat only, then eased into the bedroll. Sleep came quickly.

Raindrops jerked Fargo's eyes open. Silent lightning

flashed as it danced about in dark, ominous clouds soon to arrive overhead. While the Ovaro was accustomed to stormy weather, severe storms could panic the horse . . . and most people. As a precaution against the stallion's instinct to bolt and run for safety elsewhere, he got up and tethered it. Then he returned to his bedroll and burrowed as deep inside it as he could. He drifted asleep listening to the rain patter.

A mammoth roll of thunder shook the mountain and jarred his eyes open. He looked out. The monstrous boom reverberated in the mountains, roared and rumbled down the full length of the valley of wildflowers far below. Lightning bolts, brilliant and terrible, stabbed down from ugly black wombs in the clouds. A strong wind carrying a flood of cold rainwater set the forest canopy in violent, twisting motion. The beginning of a stream crept into the outcrop.

Fargo moved the bedroll to high ground between two shallow ravines carved by previous runoffs, now channeling this one in its downward plunge to swell the creek in the valley floor. The rhythm of the water gurgling in the ravines on both sides of Fargo put him back to sleep.

A low, throaty whinny from the Ovaro, coupled with the skittish pawings of his hooves, snapped Fargo's eyes full open. The horse was clearly signaling imminent danger. As Fargo slowly poked out of the bedroll to see what was unnerving his horse, his right hand gripped the Colt. Dawn had broken in a clear sky.

In a thicket of ground scrub less than twenty feet away stood a black bear, staring straight at Fargo. He threw the bedroll open and grabbed up a slim branch torn from a tree by the wind. Stripping away the leaves, he headed toward the bear, yelling, "Get out of here!" The surprised bear yelped as it fled to higher ground in advance of the switch beating its rump.

Fargo yawned, dropped the switch, and stretched sleep kinks from his body. He made the Ovaro ready to ride. Moments later they were picking their way up the mountainside.

In midmorning he rounded a bend. Spring Creek Pass gaped before him. There was no mistaking it; a sunray kissed off an empty whiskey bottle lying on the ground. He glanced down at the empty as he rode by, then focused his attention on the clearly defined trail that connected this pass with his main destination, Slumgullion Pass, more than eleven thousand feet above sea level.

Shortly before noon he arrived on Slumgullion Pass and reined the pinto to a halt. Jutting out of the steep slope on his right was a behemoth boulder. He dismounted, went down the slope sideways to keep from slipping and sliding, and walked out on the smooth-surfaced promontory. From that unobstructed vantage point he had a panoramic view of snow-capped San Luis Peak, which towered more than fourteen thousand feet in the east. In the west-northwest the snow-covered peak of Mount Uncompahgre, also more than fourteen thousand feet high, reached for the azure-blue sky. The white peak of Redcloud Mountain, another in the chain of gorgeous sights that rose above the fourteen-thousand-foot level, stood in the west-southwest.

It happened suddenly, without any warning, while his attention was focused on San Luis Peak. With a horrible sucking sound the moisture-laden earth all around and above the boulder churned down the steep slope. The mudslide left the boulder standing not unlike a molar surrounded by severely diseased gums that oozed vile secretions. The deadly quagmire glistened in the sunlight.

Fargo realized he was truly and hopelessly stranded. He stared down on his predicament, knowing escape was impossible.

7

A swath of earth at least fifty feet wide, beginning just below the pass, gained momentum on its downward plunge. Fargo watched the mudslide power over a ledge, cascade outward gracefully, curl, and drop. For the next minute he listened to the tons of earth, rocks, uprooted saplings, and gravel splat and bounce off terrain in its path and come to rest far below in a low place large enough to collect it.

He looked down all around his stony perch. The mire of orange-yellow clay and gray-black gravel glistened deceptively under the sun. Its slick surface was every inch of eight feet below him. To lower over the side of the boulder and drop onto it would be an act of suicide; there was no telling how deep he would sink. The slightest movement in the treacherous bog could trigger an afterslide. If none of that happened, he would still be stranded. To climb up through it was out of the question and to take the path of least resistance and go down promised a sure death when he got to the drop-off.

The top of the boulder curved down on all sides. The freshly exposed sides were rugged. The monolith stood not unlike a decaying tooth with a smooth, unblemished crown. He was in a hell of a fix. It would take days if not months of dry, sunbaked weather for a hard crust to form on the muck's surface—longer, a year or more if it rained, and it did rain here year 'round. His canteen and food were on the Ovaro, standing, waiting patiently for his return while looking down at him. Fargo wondered if the stone was to be his tomb.

He sat with his back to the pass to think his way out of the situation. A wide chasm separated him and the slopes on the other side of it. More than a hundred yards on his right was the beginning of the chasm. The peak of the inverted V emerged from the tree line and widened quickly as it carved deeply into the grassy slope. From the length of time it took the leading edge of the landslide to crash onto the bottom of the chasm, he knew it was deep. The far slope began on the ragged drop-off line about even with the one below him. Grass also grew on it all the way to the continuation of the tree line. That slope was gentler-rising than the one he was on. No less than six streams, none wide or deep, flowed out of the tree line and followed low spots to the drop-offs, where they fell as narrow waterfalls.

The mountainside above the pass rose steeply. Huge boulders, similar to the one holding him prisoner, and conifers covered it. The dense foliage prevented him from seeing the top of the mountain.

The pass curved sharply on the downside and followed the irregular contour of the mountain, wherever passage was possible. Fargo could see stretches of the trail far below. He worked backward from the lowest stretch visible from where he sat. By studying the trails he mentally constructed their probable connected route down from the pass. The uppermost stretch, which was rather long, angled at least ten degrees. It vanished in the contour at the upper end and around a rocky bend at the other. A sheer wall of gray-black rock rose behind the stretch and fell just as perpendicular below it. From what he could see of its lower end, the passage's width would accommodate nothing larger than a mounted rider. The ledge might have wider spots, he thought, but the neck of it would stop a wagon of any size. Even from the hundred yards or so from Fargo's position, it looked dangerous.

He saw no way to get off the stone and back onto the pass. He watched the waterfalls until their tedium and the sun's warmth made him drowsy. He lay facedown on the warm boulder and drifted into sleep while listening to beavers fell aspens on the far slope.

The chill in the air that came with the lowering sun awakened him. He sat up and rubbed warmth in his hands and arms. The Ovaro still stood waiting on the pass. He called to it and the horse whinnied back. Fargo knew the pinto had to be as hungry and thirsty as himself, but the faithful horse seemed to sense the problem and wouldn't leave him.

With night, rain came again. The boulder's smooth surface soon became slippery, dangerous. It behooved Fargo to sit and stay in its center. The hours dragged by. The sprinkle changed to a drizzle, which was the prelude to a wind-driven downpour. Lightning crackled in the clouds, which he now saw were the roiling type that spawned unbridled fury. He girded himself to bear the brunt of it.

The power-laden storm rolled over the mountain crest and announced its presence with fierce gusts of wind carrying ice-cold rainwater, much lightning, and earth-shaking thunder. Fargo spread-eagled himself on the boulder and clung to it for dear life. The howling wind ripped at his clothing. The driving rain stabbed icicles. He gritted his teeth. Thunder shook the stone, bounced him about, roared down the mountain and into the unseen valley far below. Lightning blasted out of the clouds. In rapid succession three trees above the pass were struck. Two in the tree line exploded. The rain-streaked chasm, watery slopes, the waterfalls, his stone, all flared garish blue-white from the bursts.

Fargo felt the boulder tilt, catch, and steady.

The storm ravished Slumgullion Pass an hour longer. The thunder and awesome pyrotechnics moved east slowly, as though reluctant to leave without destroying the mountain pass. Foreboding echoes rumbled back. They were swallowed growling by the maw, the bottomless pit that gobbled mudslides.

The wind lessened. The torrential downpour gave way to drizzle.

Fargo lay with held breath for fear his slightest movement would disturb the balance of the giant stone. He listened to the water flow over the lip of the pass, rush down against and spill around the boulder.

Dawn came painfully slow. Much earlier the wind had died altogether, but not the drizzle that cloaked the mountain and all around it. The only sound was a low whinny made by the Ovaro.

Fargo listened to the blood pulse in his temple areas.

In midmorning the drizzle still persisted. The Douglas fir and ponderosa pine above and all along the pass stood still as dripping-wet dark-green statues. Fargo peered over the edge of the boulder. The surface of the quagmire was now appreciably lower. Still lying spread-eagled, Fargo closed his eyes and willed himself to sleep. He was exhausted.

The Missouri mule, a lop-eared jack, with Seth Magee astride it rounded the bend and came onto Slumgullion Pass. Somewhere in Seth's long, shaggy dark-brown beard his chin rested on his breastbone. He was weary from loss of sleep during the night storm that caught him in Spring Creek Pass. On the tip of his nose protruded a big wart. The brim of his beaver-fur bowler hid his closed eyes. He wore a drab brown duster, ripped in two places. The red of his dirty felt shirt peaked through the unbuttoned front of the duster. So did the handle of a belt pistol with a rounded trigger guard. The weapon rode between his belt of braided black horse-tail hair and the waist of his threadbare Levi's. A rat's skull served as the belt buckle. Scuffed black boots covered his feet. A ruby-red devil's head ring encircled the third finger of his right hand. Seth stunk to high heaven.

Behind the five-foot, seven-inches tall, thirty-five-year-old bandy-legged trapper-trader trailed two of his donkeys, laden with baggage.

The jack's hesitation was brief when it saw the Ovaro standing in the drizzling rain. As it went around the pinto, Seth opened one eye. Both flew wide open when he saw the gleaming black-and-white horse. He sat erect and reined the mule to a halt. Seth frowned as he looked at the stallion and the gear on it. He scanned the pass to find the rider, then among the rocks and trees above him when he saw nobody. He dismounted and walked to the lip of the ledge and looked down.

After studying Fargo's unmoving body for a long moment, Seth went back to the Ovaro. He withdrew the

Sharps from its saddle case, looked it over, and put it back. He felt around inside the saddlebags and pulled out the folded poster. He unfolded it and fondled his unruly mustache while reading the wording and looking at the picture. After glancing toward the lip of the pass, he returned the poster inside the saddlebag. He used Fargo's throwing rope to trail the pinto from the saddlehorn on the mule. Seth climbed in his saddle and spurred the jack forward at a walk.

A rock bouncing off rock jarred Fargo's eyes open. He looked in the direction of the sound and saw it had been dislodged by the mule. The man astride the lop-eared animal had halted it to scan the rain-drenched ledge in front of him for other dangerous spots. Seth had let out enough rope so the Ovaro would have footing on the narrow ledge behind the donkeys. As Fargo came to his knees, the Ovaro looked at him and whinnied.

Fargo yelled, "Hey, mister! Over here!" He waved his arms.

Seth turned in the saddle and stared through the precipitation at him.

"Come help get me off this damn rock!" As he spoke, the boulder shifted by an inch or two, enough so that Fargo felt it. "Hurry," he added.

"Who are you? Don't lie to me!"

Jesus Christ, thought Fargo. "Skye Fargo!"

"Naw, I ain't gonna help you. You got in that fix all by yourself. You figger out how to get off."

"It won't take but a minute. Come on back and throw me a rope."

"Naw, I'm gonna leave you there. Few days out in the weather—no food or water—and you'll be weak as a kitten. No problem at all. You're a wanted man, mister." Seth laughed. "Hell, you're already in solitary confinement. You ain't going nowhere. I'll get cha on my way back."

Fargo watched the man spur his mule forward. "The little bastard means it," he muttered. The stallion whinnied again, this time shaking its head vigorously. The boulder beneath Fargo's feet twisted slightly. "Wait," he yelled. "This boulder is going to fall. If it does, mister, you'll never collect a dime on me."

Seth halted the mule. He turned and shouted, "Goddammit, mister, I cain't turn 'round here! Just hold on a damn minute. There's a place on down a ways!"

Fargo knew the man had no intention of coming back. The thieving runt wanted his magnificent pinto and all on him. Fargo could die and rot in hell before he would come lend a helping hand. "Well," Fargo muttered under his breath, "you will damn sure go to hell with me."

Fargo whistled loudly.

The Ovaro instantly dug its hooves in and backed all of the slack out of the trail rope, then put it under strain. The tension effectively locked the wet rope to the saddlehorn. The jack was jerked to a halt. Fargo whistled again.

"Giddyup, you lop-eared critter," Seth hollered. He whipped the mule's flanks with the reins. The jack tried to move forward, but the Ovaro held firm. The jack hee-hawed its near panic repeatedly. The Ovaro powered backward on the ledge. Seth continued to lash at the mule and curse it. The confused mule disobeyed and started giving ground. Seth drew his hunting knife from its scabbard on the back of his belt. Just as he positioned it to sever the taut rope, the jack bucked and knocked it from his hand. The knife caromed off the wall, pinged on the rocky outer edge of the ledge, and fell clattering off rocks en route to the bottom.

The braying donkeys backed in advance of the mule's swishing tail. Rocks on the lip of the ledge were knocked loose by the animal's hooves searching for safe ground. The powerful pinto continued to pull the mule up the ledge.

Seth, afraid one of the animals would go over the side and take the others and him with it, dismounted next to the rocky wall and plastered his back to it. The Ovaro found the mule, lighter now by 150 pounds, easy to tow steadily backward. Fargo urged his horse on by whistling to it.

First the Ovaro, then the donkeys and mule left the ledge and disappeared around the mountain's contour and from Fargo's sight. He shouted to Seth Magee, who was still marrying his back and outstretched arms to the sheer wall, "Mister, you don't have any choice now but to come give me a hand. So do it."

"You'll kill me. I know you will."

"No, I won't. Hellfire, man, I would've done the same as you. I understand! Help get me off this rock and everything will be square between us. I promise."

As he spoke, the boulder tilted a tad toward the chasm, the new angle making it necessary for Fargo to get new footing to maintain his balance on the precarious promontory.

Seth started inching his way up the ledge. He left the security of the wall about twenty feet from the upper end and ran the rest of the way. Fargo heard the donkeys braying on the pass above. The Ovaro and mule appeared on the lip.

Seth appeared next to the jack. He squatted and asked, "Whut cha want me to do? I ought to plug you."

"Don't even think about it. I've already told you I'm not mad at you. Tie the ends of our throwing ropes together. Tie one free end to my saddlehorn and toss the other down to me. My horse will have me off here and up there quick as a wink." He hoped his assuring tone would put the ugly man at ease. In an even friendlier tone, he asked, "What's your name, anyhow?"

"Seth. Seth Magee. I have a trading post down the road aways from Creede. I dunno if I ought to risk getting you off that boulder or not. I see that revolver."

Fargo sighed between clenched teeth. Magee was playing it cautious. He smelled a rat bigger than the one's skull he used for a belt buckle. Fargo dipped a hand in his pocket, worked the devil's head ring on his third finger, and withdrew it. Holding the hand out, he said, "I see you're wearing a ring like mine. Magee, we're two peas in a pod. Get the ropes."

Seth stood and pushed his hat back. His brow furrowed as he stared at Fargo's ring. "Where'd you get that?"

"Why, from Douglas Thurston, of course, same way you got yours. Get the damn ropes, Magee."

"But Howie, he said you killed Thurston and his men, Howie's brother, Pete, too. Russ will have my hide if I help you."

"No, he won't. Not after I tell him the good news. Russ wouldn't dare hurt either of us."

"What good news? Russ has a terrible temper, 'case you don't know. He killed four men in Wichita just for staring at him. Two others in Saint Joe for the same reason. One when he was a kid back in Joplin, Missouri, where he was born. Russell, he's mean. So what's the good news? It better be damn good."

Jesus, Fargo thought, this man's not just a fool, he's a pure idiot. "It's a long story, Magee, too much for right now. I'll tell you all about it on our way to Saint Lucifer. Pitch down the rope."

"What about Pete and Howie? Magee said—"

Fargo quickly cut him off when he felt the boulder move. "I had no choice. Tell you later. This boulder's about to go. Hurry, Magee, or Russ will make mincemeat out of you."

The mere thought of that possibility moved Seth Magee to join the throwing ropes and tie one end to Fargo's saddlehorn. He stood on the lip to coil the rope. Fargo got ready to catch it when thrown. The boulder tilted a few degrees more. Seth flung the coiled rope. It unwound in flight and fell too far right for Fargo to grab it. Seth gathered it back in and threw it again. This time the rope went wide left.

While he was retrieving the rope, the boulder trembled, tilted more, so much so that Fargo was forced to drop on all fours to gain traction and keep from falling. "Get it to me this time," Fargo ordered. "You can do it, Seth. I know you can." He hoped he was right, because the boulder was definitely sucking free of its soggy mooring.

As Fargo watched the coil sail high toward him, the boulder toppled.

Seth watched him slide on the smooth surface and disappear. The rope lay across the curvature of the top. There was a terrible sucking sound as the base of the monolith emerged out of the quagmire.

Fargo swung out in view, twisting and turning and with one strong hand gripping the very end of the rope.

Seth slapped the Ovaro's rump with his bowler and yelled, "Yahoo! We did it."

The boulder plunged over the edge of the chasm, Fargo into the muck. The Ovaro dragged him to safety. Fargo was covered head to foot with wet clay. He stood and extended his hand to his rescuer.

Magee was having no friendliness. "Now, what's the goddamned good news?" he said. "I've got no call to trust you, after what Howie said."

Fargo tried to avoid the subject. "I need to tell Russ first. It'll be up to him to tell others."

Magee backed up, his beady eyes narrowed. "I think you're lying to me, mister. There was lots of them rings in Walsenburg. You ain't no—"

Magee's tattered duster worked like an alarm. Fargo could hear the man's arm rustle under the heavy cloth, which also so encumbered the miner that he had no chance to raise his revolver from his belt before Fargo's bullet plowed into his shoulder. Seth went sprawling.

"You shouldn't have done that," Fargo growled. "Russ won't like it."

For a moment Seth must have thought he was lucky; the duster that had slowed him had also trapped his revolver so that it lay within his reach, under the coat.

"Don't," Fargo barked as he saw the miner try to lift the gun again. Seth Magee ignored the best advice he'd been given all day and fired.

The shot went wild, Seth's aim spoiled by his shaking arm. Fargo's shot was true. It obliterated the wart on Seth's nose, along with the nose itself and significant portions of Seth's brain.

Fargo threw the belt revolver toward the chasm, then went through the dead man's pockets. He found a plug of chewing tobacco and several matches in the shirt pocket, a flintstone, a penknife, and four silver dollars plus change in the right front pocket of the Levi's, nothing in the left. All he found in the hip pockets was a piece of paper folded twice. He unfolded it and read:

> Russ,
> I'm sending this note with some easterners going to Creede. I told the man to stop at Seth's place and give it to him. Seth, you take it to Russ. I didn't know it when Howie got with me that Douglas' wife was here in town. She's going to screw up everything for us. We can still take over Walsenburg and do what Douglas planned. I vote for you to be in charge. Bring the men fast.
>
> Carl
>
> P.S. The guy who murdered Douglas and the others. I think he knows all about Saint Lucifer. Watch out for him. He's dangerous. Rides a black-and-white pinto.

Fargo tore off the postscript, then folded and stuck the note in his hip pocket. He kept the matches and pitched everything else up among the trees above him, then sent Seth Magee's dead body over the lip of the pass.

He unsaddled and removed all tack from the mule, then swatted its rump for it to roam free. As though it could smell oats back at the trading post, the jack trotted off toward Spring Creek Pass. Fargo gave good, loving strokes to his faithful stallion, then tied the donkeys to trail it. He loosened the tie-down ropes holding the canvas to the packs, pulled the canvas back, and looked at that on the inside. One donkey carried food staples: sugar, flour, starch, and the like. The other toted a case of whiskey, twelve sticks of dynamite with fuses in place, and boxes of several different calibers of handgun cartridges. He secured the canvases back in place. Before getting in the saddle, he gulped the canteen dry and gorged himself with beans and beef jerky.

Fargo crossed the narrow ledge without incident and went around the rocky bend. The trail descended steeply. He punched out of blue spruce and onto a flat shelf that overlooked Lake San Cristobal and the valley far below. Vague though they were in the rain, Fargo knew that when viewed from here on a sunny day the scene would be gorgeous indeed. Little imagination was required see the lake mirroring a blue sky, and the valley all ablaze in nature's colors. The slopes on the far side of the lake would be shrouded in all the different colors cast by conifers and streaked with groves of aspen.

He looked down and to his left. A stream coursed down the mountain. It was damned in three places by beavers, the ponds all about the same size. Busy beavers were hard at work making a fourth farther down the stream. He heard a sapling aspen fall, then turned and left the overlook.

About halfway down the mountainside the trail entered a series of switchbacks that took him through stands of aspen and blue spruce. The twisting path led through a tight passage between angled tall rocks stabbing skyward. Several times Fargo's boots scraped the sides of the constricted pathway.

He saw the Ovaro's ears perk and swivel, his head lift higher, and he knew both warned of danger nearby. The donkeys sensed it also. They didn't want to proceed; the trail rope tightened. The pinto became nervous. Fargo looked ahead first, then up among the rocks glistening dully in the rain.

The bobcat's black-rimmed eyes met his from where the cat crouched, camouflaged on top of the rock on Fargo's left. It sprang, screaming, with all its sharp claws extended.

The bobcat landed on Fargo's left shoulder, dug its claws into his chest and back, and knocked him off the saddle. Fargo's right hand grabbed the cat's throat and held the screaming mouth and razor-sharp teeth back from slashing his neck. They fell entwined beneath the Ovaro. Fargo choked the cat as hard as he could while dodging the panicked horse's stomping hooves. The donkeys brayed their fear of the bobcat loudly.

Fargo's left hand went to his calf sheath and withdrew the double-bladed throwing knife. He muscled the bobcat beneath him, stabbed it in the side twice, then cut its throat. He dragged the cat between the Ovaro's hind legs and threw the carcass high in the rocks. No encouragement was required by him for either the pinto or donkeys to get the hell out of the rocks. Fargo wiped the stiletto's blade clean on the donkey's rump that he followed out of the rocks.

The dull-gray overcast darkened. At sunset it was once again ugly black and boiling up yet another storm that would come in the night.

Booming thunder heralded the storm's imminent arrival. It struck just as Fargo broke out of a forest of towering majestic Douglas fir and onto the east shore of the lake near its middle. Lightning bolts, too many for him to count, lit up the lake and valley. Wind howled down the length of the lake, and the rain it drove seemed impenetrable. Fargo peered to his right through the deluge.

Lightning flashed in that direction. During the brief brilliance, he saw smoke rising at the far end of the lake.

A bloodcurdling scream, ten times more terrible than the bobcat's, punctured the stormy night and wailed over the lake's choppy surface.

It was the scream of a woman in great pain . . . or fear.

8

Fargo rode at a walk along the bank toward the scream and smoke. The constant lightning bursting wild patterns in the clouds flash-painted the landscape and lake in ghostly whites and tones of gray. He rounded a bend and came out of the trees onto flat ground. Less than fifty yards in front of him he saw six wafts of smoke from as many places in a row. Coming closer and when the lightning complied, he counted six hovels in a loose semicircle on the north shore of the lake.

The woman's screams continued. Between them he heard her muted pleadings, "No, please, no . . . not again. I'll be good. I promise I will. No, oh, God, no!"

Fargo grimaced as her next piercing scream rent the downpour. Mixed in the scream was male laughter.

The hovels were arranged along this side of an elongated knoll that formed a semicircle. Two were built partway into the knoll, the others—pitiful excuses for huts—were freestanding and box-shaped. All were constructed out of sapling aspen, with no intention of permanency. Fargo wondered how the slanted flat roofs kept the rain from driving everyone outside. There were no doors or windows. Elkskin flaps covered the entrances. The smoke flowed through notched vents spaced along the top of the front walls and curled around the eaves of the roofs. Tall ponderosa pine stood behind and between the shabby lodges, none in front of them.

A horse snorted. Another whinnied. Their sounds came from the other side of the knoll.

The woman's screams and pleadings and the laughter came from the second hut from the far end of the knoll. Fargo went there and dismounted. Removing the wanted poster from the saddlebag, he listened to the screaming woman be knocked about inside the hut. He tucked the twice-folded poster inside his shirt and stepped to the donkey carrying the dynamite. He put four sticks inside his shirt and threw the others into the lake, then went to the elkskin flap. He pulled it open a few inches and looked in.

A small open fire surrounded by small smooth river rocks burned in the center of the smoky room. The single flickering flame—and it was trying to disappear—cast dancing shadows on the walls of the dim room. A stack of firewood stood just inside and left of the entrance. Two empty whiskey bottles lay on the earthen floor near the firewood. On the right side of the doorway sat a bucket of water with a dipper in it, and four tin cups on the ground. Three sticks of kindling and a saddle were on the ground this side of the circle of stones. A blackened coffeepot hung from a strand of wire over the fire. In a far corner was a partially filled bag of beans, cooking and eating utensils, and tin plates. Fargo had been inside Indian tepees far more comfortable and tidy.

One man, a tall man with broad shoulders and a strong chest, lay faceup on a bedroll spread next to the far wall. A saddle was his pillow. Fargo viewed the man's right profile through the heat waves and blue-white smoke rising from the fire. He had rugged-handsome features, black hair combed back, and his eyes were closed. A cigarette with a wisp of smoke curling from the stub of ashes drooped from the corner of his lips. He wore black clothes. A black gun belt hung from a large nail in a higher sapling above his head. The holstered five-shot, single-action Joslyn army revolver was within easy reach.

A second man, by no means as big and strong-looking as the first, sat on a bedroll, his ankles crossed and his back against the left wall. He was barely visible in the haze and shadows of the gloomy room. His saddle sat on the near end of the bedroll. His was an aquiline nose between hard dark eyes. A scar began on his forehead and ended on the left cheek after cutting through the eyebrow. He had a black beard, mustache, and unkempt wavy hair. He wore a red-and-white-checked shirt and Levi's. His gun belt hung from a nail driven high in the wall on his left. The holster held a Smith & Wesson army issue. He was watching and laughing at the third man, who was screwing the terrified female.

They were on a bedroll spread at the opposite wall of sapling aspen. The sides of their bodies to the fire glistened from their sweat mixed with rainwater leaking through the roof. Their left sides were all but hidden in the heavy shadows along the wall. The slim woman was on her elbows and knees, facing the front wall. Her small hands were balled in fists. He was on his knees behind and between hers. She was nude, and he wore his shirt only. He was a younger man, with an intense but shaven face, and blond. Both his hands gripped and held her hips to his furious lunges. Her eyes were squeezed shut. Spittle drooled from her anguish-drawn lips. Blood streaked down both cheeks from lacerations, and her left eye was badly bruised, as were both upper arms.

Fargo drew the hide covering back and stepped inside.

The man sitting drew the Smith & Wesson, pointed it at Fargo, and thumbed the hammer back, all done in one swift movement.

Across from him the man pumping the woman looked up, surprised, and froze. Her eyes flew open when he stopped abruptly, but they stayed staring at the ground between her clenched hands.

The man lying with his eyes closed neither opened them nor moved a muscle.

Fargo said, " 'Evening, gents. It's coming down like a cow pissing on a flat rock out there." He eyed the coffeepot. "Smells damn good to a man dripping wet and a mite cold." He glanced to the woman, nodded, and said, " 'Evening, ma'am," then reached down and picked up a cup.

"Hold it right there, mister," the man sitting growled. "Who the hell are you, and what're you doing here?"

As Fargo crossed to the coffeepot, he noticed the man lying open his right eye and roll it over to see him better. Fargo squatted and started filling the cup. "Skye Fargo," he said. "I'm here to deliver supplies, bring interesting news, and save your asses."

The sitter snarled, "What the hell's that supposed to

mean, 'save your asses'? From what?" He stood and glanced to the man lying on his back. "Russ, you know this guy? How about you, Elmo? Ever see him before? Ever hear of him?"

Fargo sat by the fire, warmed his hands one at a time while staring into it. He explained, "Seth caught up with me in Creede. He's under the weather, too sick to travel. He brought the supplies and had me bring them the rest of the way." He removed the wanted poster from inside his shirt and held it out to the half-naked blond.

Much to the woman's obvious relief, the blond rocked back on his haunches to unfold the piece of paper. His eyes flicked from the drawing to Fargo's face a few times, then he read it aloud and handed it to Russ. While Russ scanned it, Fargo handed Carl's note out for the gunhandler to take. He snatched it from Fargo's fingers and held it to the firelight to read.

The woman drew her knees forward and sat on her calves. She sobbed softly with her head drooped, her tangled long brown hair spilling down and hiding her face.

"Shut up that goddamn whining, you skinny bitch," Elmo snarled. "If there's anything I can't stand, it's a sniveling little whore."

She pulled her damp dress to her and worked her slender arms up through it mechanically, then drew the hem down her body slowly.

Elmo stood, entwined his fingers in her hair, and snapped her head back and up. Staring hard at her, he bellowed, "Who told you to put that on?"

"I, I . . . Please, Elmo, I'm so cold. I—"

The back of his hand slapped her mouth, splitting the lower lip. She screamed as she slumped against the saplings, then she collapsed forward and lay trembling and whimpering. Elmo kicked her quivering ass.

After reading the note, the bearded man pitched it onto Russ's chest, glanced at Fargo, and asked in a no-nonsense tone, "What interesting news?"

Fargo didn't answer right off. He watched Russ lower the wanted poster and pick up and read the note. After a long pause, Russ grunted, "Leave her alone, Elmo. And,

Frank, you can put that gun back in its holster." The eye rolled to fix on Fargo as Russ said, "Mister, you have a lot of explaining to do. It better be damn convincing."

Frank and Elmo sat, their unblinking eyes focused on Fargo's face. Russ still hadn't turned his head to look directly at him.

Fargo took a swallow of the hellaciously strong black coffee and began. "Like the note says, I killed Thurston and a few others. Now, why would I do that? Because I recognize both good and bad things when I see and hear either."

Frank grunted, "Huh, that's bullsh—"

The eye flicking his way cut him off abruptly. "Shut your mouth, Frank," Russ warned.

Fargo continued. "I knew Thurston from before, back when he went by Antoine Devereaux on Mississippi riverboats. In the Atlanta saloons before that he called himself Charles Lamont. The first time I met him he was using his real name, Claude Murdock. So, Douglas Thurston, by any name, and I go way back."

"Close, huh?" Russ mused.

"Very," Fargo replied.

"How close?"

"I was there when the Chinaman tattooed the devil's face on his chest. Close enough that he once showed me the three sixes on his left hand. Is that close enough for you?"

"Mebbe. What else close?"

The image of the petite widow lying sticky wet in bed crossed Fargo's mind. "I was, uh, shall we say very friendly with his darling wife several times . . . at his suggestion, of course."

Russ cracked a sinister grin that carried the implication he too had wallowed with her. "Go on," he muttered.

Frank spoke before Fargo could open his mouth. "Russ, he's lying through his teeth. You know he—"

The glaring eyes stopped Frank. "I told you to keep your mouth shut. Don't say another word till I say you can." His tone of voice conveyed absolute finality. It was so pronounced that Fargo believed if Frank so much as grunted, Russ would draw the Joslyn and shoot him mute forever. Frank folded his hands in his lap and stared blankly into the fire.

Fargo said, "Claude and I often talked about gaining control over a town in Colorado, what with the prospects of gold and all that comes with it. With my guns and his crooked cards and dice . . . well?" He left it hanging momentarily for their pea brains to flesh out, then went on when Russ didn't challenge or ask for an explanation. "Only thing is, one foggy night down in New Orleans he ran out on me while I was enjoying the little woman's charms.

"Later, much later, when I was in Joplin, where you were born, it dawned on me that she was in on it with him, and they planned all along to cut me out. That's why she kept me busy all night in their quarters above the saloon, so he could steal away. I'll say this for the little lady: she fooled me, acting surprised and mad as hell that he'd do such a thing."

"Simpson says she's in Walsenburg. Did you talk to her?"

"Certainly. As a matter of fact, Vanessa is the one who told me about Camp Saint Lucifer. Only thing is, she didn't know the location." Now Fargo took a risk, for he didn't know which of the townsmen was named Carl Simpson or how close the man was to Vanessa Murdock. "Carl told her about Magee and she told me. I went and got Seth, who told me how to get here."

"How come you shot Pete? Where's his brother?"

"Christ, Russ, I had no choice. They didn't know about Claude and me. They arrived in Walsenburg moments after I did. At the time none of them wore the ring. Pete tried to shoot me in the back. That snot-nosed kid they made sheriff the next day, he killed Pete, then chased after the others.

"Howie came back the next day and tried to gulch me. That's when I saw the ring on his finger. Hell, I couldn't just stand there and let him kill me, so I shot to wound him, and did. Shit, I even took him to the doctor to get patched up. The doctor said he'd be laid up for a week. I couldn't wait that long." Fargo forced a chuckle before continuing. "Neither could Howie. He left while I was asleep in the hotel. I didn't head out till after sundown. Reckoned I'd catch up to him at the trading post, but he'd already left. Howie got gunned down in a brawl over a redheaded whore in the saloon back in Creede. You know the rest."

"Not quite, mister," Russ suggested. "Now you're gonna tell me what you meant by interesting news."

Fargo refilled his tin cup with the day-old coffee. They were obviously out of fresh coffee and down to reboiling the grounds. "The kid they hung the sheriff's badge on? While he's kind of fast with a gun, he's too young and inexperienced for the job. He's still wet behind the ears. The kid's no threat.

"Vanessa Murdock and that black giant, Mozart Higgins, who follows her around, they're the threat, especially her. She has her own ideas about taking over where Claude left off." He held out his hand for them to see the ring. "She gave me Claude's ring and told me to find and bring you men to her."

He paused to glance among their faces and saw no impact of his pronouncement in the expressions. They had missed it completely, so he made it clear. Grimjawed, he spoke through clenched teeth. "Ordered me is more like it. I don't know about you, but I don't cotton to a woman bossing me around, especially when she's a pure whore."

Elmo gulped, looked at Russ, and dared to break his silence. "Goddamn, Russ, what do we do now? No woman—"

Russ held a hand up for him to hush, then asked, "All right, mister, what are you really saying?"

"Just this," Fargo began. "The people in Walsenburg think their problems are all over now that Thurston, Murdock, and his crowd are dead. Right now they're sitting around, feeling cozy, safe, and secure, figuring that punk kid sheriff can handle things. What I'm saying is, Walsenburg is vulnerable."

Fargo scanned their faces for a reaction. Russ stared at the vague, rippling fire shadows on the ceiling, Frank at the fire, and Elmo blankly at Frank. Maybe Russ was getting his drift—it was impossible to tell inasmuch as he saw only half the man's face—but Frank and Elmo . . . Well, Fargo thought, they're off in a dreamworld, not even listening.

Fargo continued. "I say to hell with the widow. We don't need her. All we have to do is ride in, shoot their baby-faced sheriff, tell her how the cow eats the cabbage, and take over. The saloon becomes our headquarters. Taking that town and those people will be easier and less noisy than screwing that woman over there." He looked at Elmo and grinned. "Wouldn't you rather have one of those shapely saloon girls?"

As Elmo broke a big agreeing smile that revealed rotten teeth, Russ posed the gut question. "Who leads?"

Fargo did not hesitate or stammer when answering, "There is but one who can do it. You. I'm out because I don't know these men, their capabilities and limitations. You do."

For the first time since Fargo came inside the gloomy room, Russ propped on his elbows and turned to face him. One fast blink was the only outer sign that betrayed the gut-wrenching knot that instantly formed and jerked in Fargo's stomach. He willed himself not to wince or stare at the disfigured left side of Russell's head and neck.

As if a line had been drawn from centerpoint on top of his head and down over the centerline of the face and neck—Fargo presumed the line continued on the backside —the right side was normal and the left severely misshapen from a searing, flesh-melting burn. It resembled biscuit dough that hadn't yet been kneaded.

There was no ear, only a horrible-looking orifice. Neither was there any hair on the ugly grayish-white scalp that had melted and solidified while sliding down. The left eye peered out of a lidless socket. There was no eyebrow, certainly not one eyelash. The lips on that side were gone, replaced by a downward-bent slit, stark white in the corner. The melted disfigurement continued down his chin and neck and ended at the collarbone.

"Are you sure?" Russ asked, then demanded, "look at me."

Fargo's eyes lifted and met Russell's. "Yes, I'm sure.

Your face doesn't bother me in the least. If anything, it's an advantage."

Russ burst out laughing insanely. Elmo and Frank cackled with him. The woman covered her ears tightly with her palms. Fargo swilled from the cup, found the rancid brew cold, and spat it onto the embers. He put two sticks of the kindling on the glowing coals and blew on them till flames appeared.

Calming, Russ said, "Advantage? I've never heard it described quite like that. Ugly, gruesome, hideous, yes, but not advantage. Until now that was my private, secret word for what Satan did to me." When Fargo's brow pinched involuntarily, Russ quickly emphasized, "Oh, yes, my big friend, Satan did it, all right. The devil marked Russell Bomar good . . . forever." Holding his gaze, he explained, "My drunk pappy shoved my head in hot coals when I was sixteen. First man I ever killed. There's been others for doing less."

"Two in Saint Joe, four in Wichita," Fargo commented, remembering Magee's revelation.

Russ chortled, "You know about them?" He glanced from Elmo to Frank. "Hear that, boys? I'm known in faraway places." He looked at Fargo. "What do they say about me?"

Fargo forced a chuckle. "They say stay out of the dough-faced man's way. They say he's Mephisto. They—"

"Mephisto?" Russ laughed maniacally. "Mephisto! Who is Mephisto?"

"I'm not sure, but I think Mephisto is one of seven devils."

"I like it," the man roared. "Perfect! I am a devil, sent straight from hell and made to scare people. The two in Saint Joe? They looked at me and their hearts stopped beating. Yes, yes, I am this Mephisto." He started the hideous laughter again.

Fargo was ready for this meeting to end and him be out of here. He rose, saying, "Then you will lead us?"

"Yes, yes!" Russ gloated in his laughter. "We'll kill, maim, rape, plunder . . . everything! I'll be glad to go, to get out of this prison of trees and mountains. Sit back down, friend. We have to plan."

Fargo squatted and said, "There's a load of whiskey on Seth's donkeys."

Elmo and Frank scrambled to their feet.

"No," Russ told them. "Have the women do it. Becky, go get the others to help you." She didn't move fast enough for him. He went to her, pushed Elmo aside, and jerked her to stand. "I said go unload those donkeys," he snarled. He muscled her to the doorway and shoved her out into the storm.

Coming back to recline on his bedroll, he spoke to Fargo. "We'll leave the women behind. Hell, they'll be glad to see us go. They're fucked out anyhow." He lay and looked at the ceiling. "We ride out in the morning, storm or no storm." A decision had been made.

Fargo silently favored it. He had no intention of staying in this hellhole long enough to see the next sunrise. He planned on being gone well before dawn broke. The others were also deep in their own thoughts. Frank kept fondling his Smith & Wesson, cocking and releasing its hammer as he stared into the fire. The only other sounds and movements in the compact room came from the flickering flames that cast hellish patterns on the saplings, and the water dripping from them.

It was different outside. Fargo listened to four female voices argue and complain bitterly while off-loading the donkey's cargo. One voice complained angrily to someone called Claudine. In rapid succession he heard the three others mentioned: Loudon, Ouida, and Jennie. So she is here, he thought. Nobody said Becky's name. She made five. He wondered how many others there were, and how many men.

Fargo looked at Elmo, who he had determined was the weakest of the three, waved his hand in front of the man's face to break his concentration, and asked, "How many of those bitching females are in camp?"

Elmo was slow to answer, as if he had to think first. "Six, right now."

"For twenty men," Frank volunteered just as slowly. "Twenty-one counting you."

Fargo studied the coffeepot while he made the probable division. Twenty men in six shacks all about the same size meant there were four bunked in each of two and three in each of the other four. And it was no wonder the women were crabby.

The door flap parted. Becky, sopping wet, labored inside lugging the case of whiskey in her arms. She set it on the ground in front of the supply of firewood and turned to go back out.

Russ stopped her. "Over here, goddammit. How many times do I have to tell you?"

She heaved the heavy box up and carried it between Russell and the fire. Setting it down, she said, "You want me to take it around or have my sisters come do it?"

Russ removed three bottles and held one to the firelight. He used a pocketknife to unplug it. "Take the rest outside and divide it among the women. Tell 'em to take it to their men."

Becky picked up the box and hurried out.

Russ tossed a bottle to Frank. Elmo waited for his, but Russ gave him an order instead. "Take our friend here and have him bunk at Reece's. Tell Reece and those with him that, rain or no rain, I want to see them at the corral at the crack of dawn. Then, on your way back, stop and tell everyone else the same thing. Tell 'em I said that, this being our last night here, it's okay to guzzle the booze. You'll get a drink when you get back."

Fargo caught his breath when he heard "guzzle." That was a big break. Elmo rose with Fargo and preceded him to the flap. Russ muttered another command, one that halted Elmo and caused him to grimace. "Tell Becky to get her skinny ass in here and suck me bone-dry."

Fargo stepped out into the downpour. He hoped it would continue unabated through the night. The worse, the better, he thought.

The six women lifting boxes and sacks off the donkeys looked like drowning rats. The eerie flashes of lightning accentuated their wet haggard appearances. One, a slim woman with narrow shoulders, was obviously pregnant. Two worked nude. None acted as if they were in any hurry to get out of the raging storm. Fargo presumed it was the lesser of two evils, well worth the cleansing, albeit damn frigid, rain. The wind didn't help.

Becky and a tall, wild-eyed black-haired female in her mid-twenties, one of the two nudes, stood on either side of the donkey immediately behind the Ovaro. Neither looked up when Fargo and Elmo came and joined Becky.

Elmo made it brief. "Becky, Russ said to tell you to come suck him off."

Her bony body straightened rigid as a steel pole. Fargo was looking at her face when a series of flashes split through the clouds overhead. Her eyes were unbelievably widened, staring so it seemed into an unclean, dark place where she'd been before and feared greatly. Her body started shaking uncontrollably. She began gulping and gasping loudly. The other women ceased bickering and turned their faces away.

Elmo nudged her in the ribs with his elbow. "Goddammit, woman, don't just stand there acting like you didn't hear me. Move your ass. Now!"

As though the word "now" was fraught with terror, Becky ran screaming toward the lake.

Cursing, Elmo chased and caught her just as she entered the cresting waves crashing ashore. He flung her back on the bank. Becky struggled to get out of his grip and, failing that, pounded her tiny fists on his chest while pleading terrified, "No, Elmo, oh, God, please, don't make me do this. Please, Elmo, I beg you to let me drown and end my misery. Plea—"

Elmo slapped back and forth across her face, snarling, "Ain't nothing to it, bitch. You don't have to look at him. Just get it over with."

Becky's eyes rolled back and slowly closed as she fainted. Her knees buckled and she collapsed. Elmo draped her over his right shoulder and headed for the donkeys.

A young blonde who Fargo guessed was still a teenager, although filled out top and bottom, broke from the crowd at the other donkey and rushed to intercept Elmo. "You bully," she yelled, "don't take her to him yet. Let me talk to her first. Dammit, she's scared to death of him." She reached to pull the limp body off his shoulder.

Elmo knocked her hands away. "Get out of my way.

This isn't any of your business. I'll take care of your little butt later. Now go take that shit inside. All of you, go back to work or I'll whip the shit out of every last one of you."

The blonde stood in his path with her hands held out in front of her. "C'mon, Elmo, give her to me . . . just for a few minutes?"

Elmo brushed past her, growled, "No. Go do what I said."

Fargo, knowing this wasn't the time to start anything, fought back the urge to strangle Elmo here and now. He forced himself to stand by helplessly awhile longer, even though it meant the poor woman would have to suffer. It would, however, be her last time, and the final time the uncaring others would have to turn their heads so they wouldn't have to watch the brutality. In truth, he thought, they shared Becky's misery, her want of death's freedom, and at the same time knew she, like them and millions of other females in bondage, was physically equipped to accept whatever sexual desire her captors demanded. Becky's was an emotional problem that stemmed from deep-seated good morals and values that could not be twisted or bent, only tortured. No amount of counseling or consoling from the blonde, or anyone else, could give Becky's torment relief.

As Elmo walked up to Fargo, the blonde made another attempt to pull Becky from his shoulder. Furious, Elmo dropped Becky to the muddy ground and grabbed the blonde's left arm. He twisted it behind her back, lifted her onto her tiptoes, and swung a fist at her face.

Fargo's hand shot out and grabbed Elmo's wrist. Surprised, Elmo snapped his head around. Fargo winked and said, "Elmo, she isn't worth the time or trouble. Russ is going to be on your ass as is for dilly-dallying. Take Becky on in to him. I've got a bottle in my saddlebags. See you at the corral." He released the hard grip he knew was hurting Elmo.

Elmo licked his lips. "Yeah, you're right." He hollered for the blonde and the others to take the supplies inside, told Fargo he would catch up to him at the corral, and pointed toward the knoll. Fargo watched him drag Becky by the hair of her head through the mud toward the hut.

Leading the pinto and donkeys to the corral, the Trailsman looked at the departing women. The blonde glanced over her shoulder at him. In her glance he recognized a bond between them had been made. She had to be Jennie Hollis, for none of the others were blonde, although he expected her to be much younger. Young though she was, she was definitely not what he would call a girl.

The sounds of Elmo mushing hurriedly through the mud preceded those of his heavy breathing that Fargo heard. Elmo darted past Fargo and lowered two rails on the corral fencing of sapling aspen. "I'll be damn glad to be shed of those whores," he said. "Goddamn, I'm happy you came and said what you did."

Fargo released the trailing rope tied to the donkey. While he coiled it, Elmo removed the rope connecting the donkeys. Fargo asked, "Is there another way to Walsenburg? Those two passes are washed out. I nearly didn't make it through Slumgullion."

"Yeah," Elmo answered easily. He pointed to an opening in a stand of aspen behind the corral. "Back that way. We call it the hidden trail. Russ marked it when he came. It's rough as hell, though. I came that way. Most of us did."

"Smart move. How did he mark it?"

"With rocks. Every now and then he lined four in a row aimed in the direction of the last four and toward where he was headed. Easy to find and follow if you know what to look for. A feller'd be in a helluva mess without those rocks. He'd get lost and wander around back in there for no telling how long. Like I said, it's rough country."

That detailed information deserved a drink. Fargo pulled a bottle of the whiskey out of a saddlebag and passed it to the informant. He watched Elmo take a long swill.

"Whooee, that's mighty good stuff," the rotted-teeth blonde claimed. His tongue swiped across his lips before he volunteered, "We been out for over a month. Seth didn't bring any last time he came."

Fargo wanted, needed other vital information, but hesitated probing for it, lest Elmo unconsciously drop it to

Russ. If any of them had the sense to smell a rat, Russ would have it. Fargo suggested, "Take the bottle with you. How about toting my saddle to where I'm bunking?"

Elmo lifted the saddle onto his shoulder and led the way. Fargo followed with the Sharps, saddlebags, and bedroll. They moved left and went to the hut on the end of the semicircle opposite from where Russell Bomar's stood.

Fargo pulled the door covering back for Elmo to enter, then followed him inside and stood the Sharps against the wall on his right. The room was almost an exact duplicate of Russell's. Only the faces were different. The three men were sitting on the edges of their bedrolls nearest the fire. The one behind the fire drank from one bottle and the other two were handing the other bottle back and forth over the fire. Jennie sat in a dark corner with her knees drawn to her chest and her arms wrapped around them. Her eyes stared into Fargo's.

Elmo dropped the saddle to the ground, grinned, and said, " 'Evening, boys. Brought you a guest for the night. Name's Fargo. He's a wanted man." His preamble stated, Elmo haphazardly aimed the bottle at each of the men as he introduced them, starting with the scrawny, thin-faced man on Fargo's left, then continuing counterclockwise. "This mean man from Ohio is Floyd Ellison. That'n back there is Reece Tatum from over in Kansas. Jenkins there, he's from Tennessee."

None directly acknowledged Fargo's presence. Jenkins grumbled something incoherent about overcrowded already. Fargo quickly sized up each man. Floyd, he concluded, was all coward beneath the thin veneer of false toughness he was trying hard to present by tensing and relaxing his facial muscles. He figured Reece a backstabber, not having the guts to take an opponent head-on. His hands gripped the bottle as if it were a dagger. And Jenkins simply looked nasty.

Elmo continued. "Boys, we're heading for Walsenburg at the crack of dawn." Their heads, and Jennie's too, snapped up. Only Jennie didn't smile at hearing the good news. "You heard right," Elmo chortled. "We're finally getting out of here. Thurston's dead. Fargo here killed him." Now their eyes cut to Fargo. Elmo went on. "Russ is leading us now. He wants everybody standing 'round the head first thing in the morning, rain or no rain. He said to go ahead and tie one on tonight, that our next drink would be in the saloon. Lots of good pussy too." He glanced at Jennie hunkered in the corner.

"Stop looking at me like that," she hissed. "You stay away from me. Reece?"

Reece muttered for her to shut up. His eyes met Elmo's. "Get out of here, Elmo. You got your own woman."

"Aw, Reece, that bawling bitch isn't no good. C'mon, pardner, lemme borrow this'n. Won't take but a minute."

Jennie shrunk deeper into the corner, drew her knees closer to her chest, and glared at Elmo.

Reece chuckled. "Don't give me that shit, Elmo. Are we taking the women with us?"

"No," Elmo replied. He grinned at Jennie and told her a terrorizing lie. "We're gonna line 'em up and use 'em for target practice."

"Thank God for small favors," Jennie sighed. "Relief comes at last."

While her words were probably uttered sincerely, Fargo nonetheless saw unmitigated fear cloud her deep-blue eyes. He wanted badly to whisper she had nothing to worry about.

"Yeah, well," Elmo retorted, "when you women are leaking blood, you'll wish you'd acted right toward us."

Reece looked at him disgustedly. "Get out of here, Elmo. Tell Russ we'll be up and ready."

Elmo cinched up his wet britches, grunted an obscenity, and left. Under the watchful eyes of the men, Fargo spread his bedroll on the doorway side of the fire and laid his saddlebags between it and the bedroll. Floyd, he noticed, was eyeballing the bottle held at Jenkin's lips. Fargo retrieved another bottle of whiskey from the saddlebag and handed it to Floyd, saying, "Kill it, pardner. I've been sucking on the stuff all day to stay alive while coming down that mountain in the storm. If there's any left in the morning, I'll finish it off."

Floyd eagerly accepted the bottle. He even let the facial muscles relax for good and smiled and nodded to

Fargo. "Won't be any left," Jenkins volunteered. "Once we start, we don't stop till it's all gone."

Fargo hoped the three bottles would be enough to souse their brains in short order. He pulled his boots and clothes off and slipped into the dry bedroll. He closed his eyes and faked sleep while listening to them drink as he watched the flickering colors cast by the fire penetrate onto the inside of his eyelids.

Shortly, he heard movement on Jenkin's bedroll. It sounded like the man was undressing. Jennie's voice complained, "Oh, God, no, Jenkins. Not again. Please, not now. I'm too tired. Besides, I don't feel good."

Reece slurred, "Don't argue, Jennie. Do what he says and shut up. I'm coming in after him. Want thirds, Floyd? Last time for a spell."

"Why not?" Floyd answered, thick-tongued.

The sounds of Jennie softly crawling onto the nasty man's bedroll pounded into Fargo's ears. He heard raw flesh unite, her groan, "Oh, God, hurry. You're killing me. Please hurry and get it over with."

Jenkins' reply came out garbled from liquor, but his slap on Jennie's back was clearly heard. While listening to him grunt and her groan painfully, Fargo squinted at Floyd and Reece.

Floyd leaned awkwardly against the saplings and had difficulty keeping his fluttering eyes open. The eyeballs were wandering, rolling of their own accord. An unfeeling hand rested on the neck of the near-empty bottle on the bedroll between his parted legs. Floyd was moments away from entering a swirling world of darkness complete with numbness.

Reece sat rocking slowly from side to side, obviously unable to stop the swimming sensation backstroking in his brain. His eyes were already closed. Fargo watched Reece's hands relax open. The empty bottle rolled out on the bedroll. It all promised Reece was now deaf, dumb, and blind.

Jenkins grunted, "I think I'm com—"

He never finished the word or deed. Fargo glanced over his shoulder when he heard flesh smack the earthen floor. Jenkins had collapsed backward. He lay still with his legs apart, Jennie's knees between them. Fargo turned slightly and looked into her watching eyes and shot her a wink with a grin. He brought a finger to his lips, indicated for her to stay quiet and not to move.

Slowly he came up to a sitting position and waved his hand before Floyd's face. The man neither moved nor blinked. He studied Reece's face for a sign of awareness. Reece was out cold. Blubbering soft snores spilled from the dark corner where Jenkins' head lay. Fargo stood, gestured for Jennie to do likewise, and started pulling on his clothes. She shrugged, splayed her palms, and motioned that Jenkins was lying on her dress. Fargo waved to her that it didn't matter, then nodded for her to get his bedroll. While he collected the saddlebags and his saddle, she quickly rolled the bedroll and tied it up. He nodded toward the door. She went out first.

He hugged her to him while going to the corral. "Jennie, we don't have much time. Your father sent me to get you out of here." When she looked at him questioningly, he asked, "You are Jennie Hollis, aren't you?"

"Uh . . . sure, I am," she replied haltingly. "How is Daddy and my mother? He sent you?"

"Your mother's worried sick. They both are. I've never met either of them. He sent Kid—"

"Ballas," she butted in.

Any apprehensions Fargo may have had about her not being the rancher's daughter disappeared when she mentioned Kid's last name. They said nothing more till Fargo was making the pinto ready to ride. Then he said, "I hope you women know how to ride bareback and without reins."

"Mister, riding bareback is what we do best. God knows they've given us plenty of experience. I know I can. The others will be so happy to leave this godforsaken place, they'll learn in the first fifty yards."

"Now you're going to tell me about the women, what to expect from each. Start with their names and which shack they're in."

"Becky Tayler you know about. She's on the verge of going crazy."

"Go on."

"As for me, you can count on me to do whatever you want, whatever is necessary to help us escape."

"Can you handle a rifle?"

"Certainly. I'm a crack shot."

He handed her the Sharps, a fistful of extra cartridges, and showed her how to load and eject. "It's got a nasty kick," he said through an easy grin. "We'll take care of the shoulder bruise later."

Now she grinned. "Mister, all of us are covered with bruises."

"The gunfire is going to get hot and heavy once I make my move. You're going to pin them inside from where you will lie to shoot from behind that devil's head. I'll be busy doing other things. You'll see me, so for Christ's sake don't aim at me. What about the other four?"

"Nancy Phillips, the pregnant girl, is in the hut at the other end from Reece's. She's been here the longest. Frank Selman brought her with him when he came with Russ. You best not expect much out of Nancy. Actually, in her condition she will be in the way. There's four men in with her: Zack River, Axel Po—"

"Forget their names. Just tell me how many are in each hut."

"On the other side of Russ's is Claudine Wellfort and four men. Claudine will be a problem. She's already half-crazy. There's no telling what she might do.

"Next to her are three men and Loudon Franklin. Now Loudon is tough as a prospector's boot. She's Indian-wild. Utes had her six years. She'll fight, so you can count on her being right in there with you.

"On the other side of me in Ouida Thompson and three men. Ouida's the oldest of us. She's twenty-nine. Got a tongue sharp as a knife. She argues and complains a lot, but I think you can look for her to do what you say. What else?"

"Nothing. I think I have a clear picture of what I'm up against. You have about ten rounds. Girl, make each count, bury each in flesh. A wound is as good as a kill, maybe better. So hit something soft that bleeds."

"Balls?"

"Too small a target. Go for the heart."

The Ovaro stood ready for the trail. Fargo selected six horses and separated them from the others. He had her keep the six at one end of the corral while he took the others to the opening behind the corral and chased them into the wet forest.

They returned to the shack. Reece and the others hadn't moved. All were now snoring. Fargo withdrew his throwing knife and stepped to Floyd. With his left hand poised to pull the head back and the stiletto positioned to slash the exposed throat, he waited for thunder to mask Floyd's dying gasp, should he make one. Jennie averted her eyes. Thunder rumbled. Fargo yanked the head back and slashed wide and deep. For an instant Floyd's eyes bulged wide open, then they closed.

Fargo moved to Reece and repeated his actions. Reece's choking sounds from his own blood were lost in the thunder. Fargo lay him on his side and went back to Jennie. He held the stiletto out for her to take by the handle. In her ear he whispered, "I'm giving you Jenkins for what he did to you."

She looked at the gleaming stiletto, gulped, and whispered back, "I don't know if I could actually do it. He deserves it, yes, but he's a huma—"

Fargo took the Sharps and cartridges from her and put the stiletto's handle in her palm and closed her fingers around it. He whispered, "Try. I'll be right there behind you. Don't worry if he hollers. There's nobody but us to hear." He took his hand away and nodded for her to go ahead.

Jennie stared at Jenkins' supine position. Fargo watched her gaze lower and halt on his crotch. She glanced into Fargo's eyes. Hers flared, as though suddenly seeing a dreadful image in her mind. Her breathing quickened. She gulped again and looked back at Jenkins. Fargo waited, knowing she was wrestling with her conscience. She took a step toward Jenkins and halted. Fargo believed she couldn't go through with it. He reached to relieve her of the stiletto.

Jennie jerked her hand away, took another cautious pace, then fell atop Jenkins and sliced upward from his crotch to navel. Jenkins' eyes flew open. His mouth gaped to scream. Fargo moved to put a swift end to it, but before he could take the stiletto from her, she cut Jenkins' throat wide open, buried the stiletto in his stomach, twisted it violently, and left it there. She rose with her knuckles pressed to her mouth and backed into Fargo's waiting arms. He held her tense back tight against his chest. They looked down at Jenkins' bloody body.

In his normal voice, Fargo said, "The first time to kill is always the hardest. Now you will find it easy not to shut your eyes or be afraid when you kill with the Sharps. Put your dress on and let's go do what has to be done to finish this mess."

Jennie tugged her bloodstained dress from under Jenkins and slipped it over her head and down her nakedness. Fargo withdrew the knife, wiped it clean on Jenkins' bedroll, then sheathed it. He handed her the Sharps and cartridges. They turned to leave.

The covering flew back. Russ, the big drifter, Scarchin, and Frank Selman stood in the opening. All held whiskey bottles. Scarchin had the wanted poster wadded in his free hand.

Frank, Russ, and Fargo drew their revolvers at the same time.

9

Before any of them could fire, a monstrous bolt of lightning struck and exploded on the knoll behind the structure. The deafening blast shook the ground violently beneath their feet and lit up Camp Saint Lucifer extra-brilliant.

The sounds of the three weapons firing together were lost in the loud crack of the lightning. Russell fired while tottering. The bullet screamed by Fargo's left ear and chewed into a back wall sapling. Also off-balance, Frank obviously jerked the trigger. His slug threw coals from the fire pit. Fargo shoved Jennie clear and fired the Colt. The slug buried in Scarchin's upper right thigh. He yelped and moved to his right. Bomar and Frank fled left.

Keeping the Colt moving left to right across the doorway, Fargo told Jennie, "When you hear me yell, run and get in your position." He backed up to the fire, ran, dived through the doorway, and slid several feet on the muck.

Rolling to his right, he fired blindly, hoping to hit Bomar or Frank. He heard no killing thud. They shot back, both bullets whizzing past where his chest would have been had he not dived. The wounded outlaw also fired at him. The bullet squished into the mud near Fargo's head. He swung the Colt around to shoot, but the man darted to safety around the corner of the shack. Cutting his eyes back to the other corner from where Bomar and Frank had fired, he saw they too had disappeared around it.

Fargo sprang to his feet, shouted, "Now!" He went after Russell and Frank. With his back to the front wall, he quick-peeked around the corner. It was too dark for him to spot them. He waited for lightning to flash.

Jennie raced through the storm and belly-flopped behind the big devil's head. The Sharps started barking, the slugs chewing into front saplings on her targets.

Fargo heard Bomar and Frank shoot at her from where they were somewhere between him and the next hut. He glanced to the far corner to check on the big outlaw, saw he wasn't there, then stepped out to duel with Russell and Frank. Lightning flashed. Fargo saw them running onto the knoll behind the next hut.

Cowards, Fargo thought. They're heading for their horses. He dashed toward the front of the adjacent hovel. Halfway there, the wounded outlaw shot at him from atop the knoll behind Reece's shack. Fargo swung the Colt around and fired twice. The slug's impact hurtled the wounded man off the rise and down its far slope.

Fargo continued running. As he passed in front of the hovel built partway into the knoll, he fired two rounds into the doorway to hit or intimidate those inside. He sped around the corner and raced through the open space between it and the next lodge, also built partway into the knoll, to intercept and prevent Bomar and Frank from getting their mounts.

As he came up on the knoll, lightning flashed and he saw them bending to go through the corral railings; they saw him too. They abandoned the railings and ran away from Fargo, toward their shack, staying between the corral and the knoll. They were quickly swallowed in the dark and heavy rain and lost from Fargo's sight. He let them go.

Fargo pulled one stick of dynamite from inside his shirt, lit the short fuse, and pitched it toward the hovel next to Reece's shack. He leapt from the knoll and landed next to the corral just as the explosion ripped the night. He reloaded and moved down alongside the corral and stopped after passing behind the other hovel half-jutting from the hillock. He lit another fuse and flung the stick over the hill toward the hovel, waited for the blast, then scrambled up the rise and came atop it between the smoking hovel and the shack next to it.

Thunder rumbled in from over the lake. Loud cracks of lightning and their blinding flashes zigzagged in the roiling black clouds. Two women and their drunken tormentors stumbled out of the two smoking abodes and collapsed in the mud. Jennie continued to lay down fire on the three shacks at the west end. Fargo didn't see Bomar or Frank.

He sprinted west among the aspen on the knoll and stopped when he came even with the west side of the nearest shack. Bomar and Frank had their backs plastered to the wall near the front corner. They sprang from the wall just as he fired. They ran in a crouch behind the next shack, firing blindly at him all the way. The darkness, compounded by the deluge, shielded them. Fargo moved along the top of the knoll to maybe spot them.

The three wobble-legged desperadoes inside the third hut from the west end came out firing wildly at Jennie and ran to follow Bomar and Frank. The woman inside with them ran out screaming and dived headlong into the mud.

Thinking Bomar and Frank might have been stupid enough to run in and join Elmo, Fargo lit a fuse and hurled the stick of dynamite toward Russell's shack. It hit on the roof and bounced over the far side. The blast caved in the wall and the roof fell in.

Concurrent with the jolt, the four men in the end shack emerged and ran, loop-legged from liquor, for safety at the river. The pregnant woman staggered outside and simply stood there. Becky crawled from the debris of the shack that had caved in.

"All the women are out and alive," Fargo muttered. He glanced to the river, now knowing Bomar and the other survivors were hidden on the downside of the bank. Fargo shouted to Jennie, "Bring the women to the corral!"

A fusillade of bullets answered from the riverbank. Most went way high and ripped through the aspen leaves.

Fargo fired back to keep them pinned down and buy time for Jennie and the other women hurrying to the corral. As they came over the knoll behind him, he told Jennie, "Get them on horses and get the hell out of there. Hurry. I'll hold off the bastards as long as I can."

He kept the Colt's barrel hot until he saw the last of the women ride out of the corral and head for the opening behind it. Much lightning exposed their hasty departure.

Bomar and his gang sprang from their positions and laid down a blistering volley of gunfire in Fargo's direction. Fargo ran down the side of the knoll, vaulted the top railing, and leapt into his saddle. He lit and threw his last stick of dynamite as far down on top of the hump as he could, then spurred the Ovaro to jump over the rear railings, yelling, "Boy, go!" The powerful stallion tucked its forelegs, cleared the railing by two feet, and charged into the pitch-black opening.

While Fargo couldn't see them for the rain, he heard the women's mounts pounding, flying with the wind eastward through the tall forest of Douglas fir. He came alongside Jennie and told her, "For the moment we're safe. That'll change when they round up their horses and sober enough to stay in the saddle. You watch the rear. I'll ride on up and lead the way."

"I have only one extra bullet left," she said, urgency in her voice.

"Then make it count." He spurred the stallion forward.

Passing the pregnant woman, he slowed and asked, "You doing all right?"

She held a tight grip on the horse's mane. "Mister, I'm so damn glad to be doing this that I wouldn't notice it if I started having my baby."

He grunted and plunged ahead. The continuing lightning showed the way among the trees. He spotted the first row of four stones ahead. He dismounted and threw them away. The hard rain would destroy all indications of where they had been, and wash away all signs left by the horses. If Bomar or one of his men was a first-class tracker, they would be able to follow the trail, but not at a fast pace.

Occasionally, Fargo looked over his shoulder to see how the women were doing. Fear or talent—he didn't know which—had them riding like they'd been reared on bareback horses. He kept the fast pace awhile longer, then slowed to a trot and finally to a walk. A half-hour deeper into the forest he reined the pinto to a halt and dismounted.

The women slid off their mounts. During a flash of lightning, he saw most rubbing their butts and chuckled. "Yeah, ladies, you didn't think you had any feeling left, did you? Well, it'll get worse before it gets better. This time tomorrow your seats will be raw, so raw it will hurt to walk. You get fifteen minutes on the ground, then it's back in the saddle."

"What saddle?" three voices chorused disgustedly.

Fargo cupped his hands and let them fill with rainwater. The women did likewise.

Ouida asked, "When do we eat?"

The others looked at him and waited to hear the answer. "I'll catch a fish and break a loaf the next time the sun comes out." He watched their eyes bat. He stepped to the pregnant woman. "Your name is?"

"Nancy Phillips."

"Nancy, from here on you ride my stallion."

"That's not necessary. I can ride like the others."

"I'll change horses with you," Ouida volunteered. She sounded and looked serious.

"No," Fargo replied, "Nancy gets the saddle."

Fargo boosted Nancy up in the saddle. Her expression conveyed it was far more comfortable than the previous spine that attacked her crotch. She nodded her thanks.

"Mount up, ladies," he told them. "The devils could be right behind us." No other words were needed. Manes were grabbed, legs hiked, and they rolled up on the horses' backs.

Fargo led with his mount at a walk. He found and destroyed several rows of the marker stones. They rode until he stopped at dawn, when the trailing edge of the storm passed overhead. He halted near a pond fed by a waterfall. Huge smooth boulders framed the pond on two sides.

The women were accustomed to frigid baths and being seen nude. Two—he thought their names were Claudine and Loudon—shucked their dresses before dismounting. Fargo helped Nancy to the ground. She pulled her dress up and over her head as she walked to the pond. Fargo took the Sharps and went looking for something large to eat.

Twenty minutes later Becky, who lay warming her naked back on one of the boulders, saw him returning with an eight-point buck across his shoulders. She sat up and told the others. They gawked momentarily, then left the water and boulders and came to him.

Loudon, who had lived with Ute captors so long, took charge. "Lay it on the flattest boulder," she told him, "and give me your knife. Jennie, you and two others build a cooking fire. The rest of you can help me."

Fargo lowered the buck on the stone, then stared at it. He gave up his knife reluctantly. Frowning, he asked, "Er, uh, what do you want me to do?"

Loudon made the first cut, answering, "Sit and wait. This is woman's work. We'll take care of things."

Ouida snapped an alternate suggestion. "Go catch that fish."

Fargo sat on the bank downstream and thumped pebbles across the creek. He watched a pair of hummingbirds move among the wildflowers in a small clearing on his right. Tiny wrens couldn't make up their minds which side of the creek they wanted on. A whistle pig rooted in the underbrush behind him. He got up and moved to lie on one of the stones while waiting.

The women knew what they were doing. He noticed Jennie and her helpers had worked wedge-shaped rocks into dead tree trunks, then pounded on the wedges with large stones until the trunk split. They used only the dry wood from the inner core to build the fire. There was virtually no smoke to reveal their position.

Within moments a spit laden with cuts of venison stood straddling Jennie's fire. Nancy and Becky took turns rotating the spit. Ouida and two others walked the creek banks. They came back with berries in the cradles they made by holding up the front hems of their dresses.

Theirs was one of the best trail meals Fargo had ever eaten.

Claudine mused, "Have we gotten away? I guess I mean, do you think they will come after us?"

Fargo swallowed a bite of the delicious meat. "Oh, they will come, all right. There's no longer any reason for them to stay back there. Whether they come this way or go through Creede, I don't know. But they will ride for Walsenburg. By noon we should know which way they chose."

Loudon cut squares out of the deerskin for each of the women and Fargo. After eating, the frugal woman sliced strips from the remaining cooked venison and divided them among the squares. She folded the corners in, then tied the bundles with sinew.

The fire was doused with water from the pond and the residue scattered among dense foliage well away from the site. When they were finished, it was as though a fire or seven people had never been there. Pleased with their teamwork, especially Loudon's leadership—Fargo made a mental note to put her in charge of their future campsites—he had them mount up and head out toward the sun.

At high noon, he dropped back to change mounts with Nancy. "What say you ride this hard spot for a while?" He nodded toward the mountain on their right. "I want to go up and have a look behind us."

"Mister, I'm used to hard things. Help me down."

She held his shoulders and he her waist. He paused in the lowering and looked into her sad eyes. He could only imagine the hell she went through these past months, an experience that would haunt her to the end of her days. He wanted to say something that would wash it away, but he couldn't find the words. He lowered her to the ground. She looked at him briefly, then got on the horse. In her eyes Fargo thought he saw a message that might have said, I'm all right. He eased into his saddle and reined the Ovaro right.

He went high and found a ledge that provided a clear view of the valley below in both directions. It felt good to be alone again, just him and the Ovaro and the wilderness; Fargo was in his element, and he knew it well.

He first scanned the valley behind the tiny forms of the women and horses. He saw no smoke lingering from a campfire, and Bomar's would have had to be larger than the women's. He focused on the fartherest clearing visible from the ledge. Seeing no movement, he shifted to the next clear area and observed it for a while. He saw nothing amiss. He viewed all the open spots and found nothing to make him believe they were being followed. He concluded the men were either so far behind that they would never catch up to the women, or they had opted for Creede.

Fargo maneuvered the pinto down the mountainside and into the valley. Moments later he galloped up to Jennie who was bringing up the rear. "See anything?" she asked.

"Got an eyeful of splendid landscape. They aren't behind us."

Her cheeks ballooned. She released the big breath she held and smiled. "God, there is a heaven, after all."

"Yes," he agreed quietly. "Unfortunately we are tested many times in many different parts of hell before we get there. Walsenburg will be the site of the next test."

"Fargo, you make it sound so final."

"For some it will be."

Her lips formed into a naughty smile. "Fargo, tonight spread your bedroll away from the light of the fire. I want to show my appreciation."

He considered her full rump and bouncing breasts, wishing Jennie wasn't the daughter of the man who paid and sent him to return her home safely. "Can't do that," he replied.

"Why not?" she complained.

He hedged, saying, "It would be unfair to the others."

She looked at him and blinked. He galloped the Ovaro to Nancy and swapped mounts with her.

"Are they coming?" she asked, much concern in the tone.

"No. You and the others can relax."

He rode ahead and scouted for markers.

At sundown on the fifth day they came to the sand dunes west of Sangre de Cristo Mountains. He halted the weary women and their horses. As everyone dismounted, he noticed none rubbing feeling back into their buttock cheeks. All soreness and rawness had disappeared. Now they were trail-toughened.

He looked toward the mountain range and said, "Ladies, we have one more hill to climb, then it's all downhill to Walsenburg."

10

Fargo followed the line of bareback riders into Walsenburg from the west and onto Dynamite Street. Behind them the sun was lowering, swallowed up by storm clouds they had watched build since noon, the reason Fargo had kept them moving without letup. "Some of you are in no condition to ride out another big storm," he had told them. "Your mounts would bolt and scatter. We would never find them, much less catch them. And, my darlings, on foot you would surely perish."

Neil Kaspar appeared in the entrance of his stable. Amused by the old man's gawking at the bare legs hanging down, Fargo grinned. Kaspar stiffened and rubbed his eyes when the black-and-white pinto with a full-bellied female in the saddle walked by. Fargo rode on a dun mare behind her. He waited for Kaspar to take disbelieving eyes off Nancy and look his way before speaking.

"How's things going, old man?"

Neil rushed out, saying, "Well, I'll be damned." He continued as he walked alongside the dun. "Glad you're back, son. Where'd you get all these tired-looking women?"

So, Fargo thought, now he's calling me son. "Well, Pops, guess you could say I let them out of a prison of sorts. Is Kid Ballas back?"

"Nope. Leastwise I ain't seen him if he is. Why? You expecting trouble?"

"It's coming, and I don't mean the storm. Can't say when, though."

"Oh? What kind of trouble?"

"The kind with guns and bullets. Fetch Swede and Hushour and the three of you meet me at the café. I'll explain what's to be done." Excited, the old man moved to go do it. Fargo stopped him, asking, "Where will I find Carl Simpson?"

"Carl? He's the piano player."

Fargo nodded. Neil Kaspar hurried down the street. Fargo rode past him and came alongside Jennie leading the procession. "Go right at the intersection," he informed her. "You'll see the café on the left next to the Buckhorn Hotel. Have them go inside the café and order anything they want. Mention my name and that I'm paying. I'll join you after making arrangements for rooms at the hotel."

He angled toward the hotel. The reinless dun was left to roam when he dismounted and went inside.

Freida looked up from paperwork on the counter. "Mr. Fargo, I'm so happy to see you again, and I know Ben will be also. He's visiting at the Schuttes' right now." She turned the journal for him to sign.

Fargo touched the brim of his hat. "Thank you, ma'am. Glad to be back. I need six rooms."

"Oh, me," she replied, disturbed. "Mr. Fargo, two rooms are all we have vacant."

"I'll take them." He signed his name on the bottom two lines. She handed him the keys. Heading for the front door, he said, "When Ben comes back, would you ask him to meet me at the saloon?"

"Of course, Mr. Fargo."

Crossing to the saloon, he saw the sign out front had been removed and no lamps burned inside. Neither were any horses hitched to the long twin rails. Vanessa Murdock was obviously doing exactly what she said.

He entered the dark room and went behind the bar. The distinct odor of fresh paint permeated the room. He noticed the mirror had also been taken down. Opening a bottle of what he hoped was bourbon, he glanced at the dim light that came from below the office door down the short hallway. The soft sound of bare feet moving about in an upstairs room drew his gaze to the top of the stairs. The upper level and hallway were pitch-black. He swigged from the bottle of whiskey while stepping to the office door. He entered without knocking.

Vanessa stood at the hearth warming her backside

when his quiet entrance caught her saying, ". . . first thing in the morning." Surprised, she looked away sharply from Mozart, who lounged in one of the sofa chairs facing her, then she broke a wide smile when she recognized Fargo. Mozart turned his huge head and followed her gaze. She wondered aloud, "How on earth can a man your size be so soft-footed? Come inside, Fargo, and have a seat. We're discussing what to do tomorrow."

Fargo sat in the other sofa chair. After drinking from the bottle, he said, "If it looks as fresh out there as it smells, you have done wonders in so short a time. 'Evening, Mozart."

Mozart nodded.

She said, "I've ordered a new mirror and sign from a place in St. Louis. Swede has the framework up on our new quarters out back. The paint out in the saloon should be dry enough for me to let people in tomorrow. Did you find Saint Lucifer?"

The question drew his gaze onto the leering devil's head enveloped in the flames. "That's what I came to see you about. I'll explain it later, but right now, Vanessa, I have a problem I need you to solve."

"Will if I can," she replied.

"I have six exhausted ladies in the café, eating the first decent meal they've had in God only knows how long. Months. I need—"

Mozart gasped, "Six?"

"From Saint Lucifer?" Vanessa wedged in.

"Yes," Fargo confirmed. "I need a place for three of them to spend the night. The hotel has rooms for two of them. Could those three stay here?"

"By all means, Fargo, bring them over. I have one empty bed. The other two can share with two of the girls. But that's only five. What about the sixth . . . and yourself?"

"One's foot-broke and shouldn't be climbing up and down stairs. I'll figure it out. I'll stay with Neil Kaspar."

"Oh, no, big man, I'm not letting you bunk with that old man. Uh-uh, not when I have a big warm bed for you. You're sharing my bed."

Fargo cleared his throat, tipped the mouth of the bottle to his, and said, "I need to hold a brief meeting with some of the men tonight. I am taking the liberty of inviting them to the saloon."

"Fine with me," she answered quickly, "if they can stand the smell. Mozart, light all the lamps and have the girls dress and come down. Anything else, Fargo?"

"No, not for now." He rose and left the room. Going through the doorway, he glimpsed a man go out the back door. He frowned, now remembered the eavesdropper's silhouette matched that of the skinny piano player's, and he gave chase with the Colt in hand.

Carl Simpson ran, weaving through Swede's framing, as if the devil himself chased after him. Fargo, not having seen the framing before, had problems getting through it, and getting off a shot at the fast-moving piano player was impossible.

Simpson vaulted the corral fence behind Hushour's bathhouse, sprung onto a saddled horse, which knocked off the top railing when Carl spurred it to jump out of the corral. It happened too fast for Fargo to get off a shot.

The Trailsman vaulted the fence and rushed to the street side. Carl had the horse in a dead run, fleeing into the night at the west end of Dynamite Street. Fargo watched him disappear, uncocked the Colt, and crawled through the railings. He headed for the café.

He sat on a counter stool and faced the women sitting at the window tables. Millie's head and shoulders poked through the archway so she could see who came in.

"Give me the biggest steak you have," Fargo ordered. "Potatoes, and some of everything else you have back there. But first, pour me a cup of that delicious coffee I smell."

"Anything else, big man? And I do mean, any *thing*." He heard her fill a cup and set it on the counter behind him.

"How's your husband, Millie?" he said by way of rebuke without glancing over his shoulder.

"He's not with us anymore. The day after you left, he died. His appendix busted. Doc Williamson couldn't save him. So, now do I have any *thing* you'd love to have?"

"The steak cooked on the rare side."

Millie stalked to her kitchen. Several of the women chorused a snicker.

To the women Fargo said, "After we eat, I'm taking all of you across the street to the bathhouse. After you're scrubbed clean, Jennie, you and Becky have rooms in the hotel. The saloon across the street is closed for remodeling, but I've talked to the owner and she's agreed for the rest of you to sleep in the rooms upstairs. All, that is, except Nancy. Nancy, I'll walk you to Doc Williamson's and put you under his care in one of his spare bedrooms."

Nancy started to speak.

Before she could, Millie appeared in the archway and said, "No, she isn't. We've already discussed it. She's staying with me till the baby comes." Her tone of voice was filled with finality.

Fargo looked at Nancy, who verified they had indeed made such an arrangement. "Mr. Fargo, while I appreciate your kind offer and concern, I do prefer staying with a woman. I'll help Millie here in the café to repay her generosity."

With that obviously settled, Fargo sipped from his coffee.

Kaspar, followed by Swede and Hushour, came through the door. Swede and Hushour took stools on either side of Fargo and riveted their full attention on him. Kaspar went behind the counter and filled three cups with coffee. As Fargo spoke, Millie started serving platters heaped with food to the hungry women.

"Gents," Fargo began, "I want you to fan out and bring every man who can handle a gun and isn't afraid to stand and fight to the saloon. All hell's going to break loose in Walsenburg. The town needs to get ready to fight for its life. I'll explain everything later in the saloon." He looked at Hushour. "Fred, these womenfolk are in need of baths. Okay to use your tubs? I'll stand guard at the gate."

"Sure," Fred replied, glancing at the eating females. "I don't have any customers. You want me to stoke the coals before I help Neil and Swede round up men?"

"Not necessary. I'll do it. Drink up and get out of here. I'll see you in the saloon."

They gulped down their coffee and left.

Ouida complained from around a mouthful of fried chicken, "I don't like it. I just came out of one whorehouse and here you are sticking me in another one.

Seems like I ought to have some say-so. Move sweet Jennie or Becky to the saloon so's I can have a decent room in the hotel."

"No," Fargo said sternly. "The arrangements have been made. If you or anyone doesn't like it, then it's fine with me. You can find your own place to sleep."

Millie set the platter overlapped with a T-bone before Fargo. Placing bowls of mashed potatoes, cream gravy, and black-eyed peas beside the platter, she remarked. "You're a hard man, Fargo. Let them decide who stays where."

Fargo stared hard into her eyes. Millie gulped as he said, "What I say goes. Don't ever forget that. None of you. My responsibility doesn't end till the men from Saint Lucifer are dead. After that, they can do what they well damn please, not before." He carved off a bite of steak and poked it in his mouth.

Millie cleared a frog stuck in her throat, picked up the coffeepot, and started refilling cups. Neither Ouida nor anyone else challenged his authority.

After eating, he escorted them to the bath area. Without any shame or reluctance, they started undressing while he stoked the coals to bring up the heat. He stood back and watched them divide, go up the steps, and ease down in the water. As each did, a grand sigh escaped through her lips. They slipped down until only their heads showed over the rims of the tubs.

Becky whispered, "I may never come out."

When they were done, Fargo gave them new instructions. "Next stop is the meeting in the saloon next door. I'll escort Jennie and Becky to the hotel, then join you. Nancy, you can go to the café."

On the way to the hotel he detoured to the Ovaro hitched to a post between the hotel and café. Nancy paused before opening the café door and looked at him. She smiled and waved while he was removing the saddlebags, bedroll, and Sharps. He nodded to her, then carried his stuff to join the two women standing on the hotel's porch.

Freida tensed when she saw Fargo lead the two bedraggled women into her lobby. Fargo smiled as he passed her. Upstairs, he unlocked Number 8, swung the door open, and scanned the dark room before entering. The two females waited at the door until he lit the lamp and beckoned them inside. "Who wants it?" he asked.

"She does," Jennie answered. "Don't you, Becky?"

Becky nodded, sat on the edge of the bed, felt over it, then grinned her pleasure and bounced on it a couple of times. "Thank you, Mr. Fargo," she sighed. "The trip was worth the hardships." She swung her legs up onto the bed and stretched out.

Fargo pitched the room key onto the bed. He shut the door and led Jennie to the room where he'd stayed. She followed him inside and sat on the bed while watching him light the lamp. He stood the Sharps against the wall next to the bed and put a handful of cartridges beside the lamp. "Just in case," he explained. She watched him put the saddlebags on the seat of the chair and his bedroll on the floor next to it. "You can look after them also. I'll come get them when I'm ready to leave town."

He started for the door. She hopped off the bed and intercepted him. Embracing him, she whispered, "Come back and stay with me after your meeting. I want to show my thanks in a special way. Will you?"

He wasn't about to make love with the rancher's daughter. The man had paid him to deliver her, not what she was clearly suggesting. He hedged the problem. "Maybe. Can't say for sure. This meeting might last all night. If you hear the door open, it will be me."

She looked up into his eyes. Hers were filled with expectancy. She smiled. "I'll be waiting, darling, with open arms and open . . ." She let it trail off, the ending promise implied.

He kissed her on the cheek, dropped the room key on the bed, then turned and left. Freida registered surprise when he came down the stairs alone . . . and so soon. He touched the brim and said, "Good night, ma'am. See you tomorrow."

Fargo deposited the Ovaro at the livery and headed to the saloon. He paused in the hallway opening to see who was present. Mozart had lit all the lamps. The white walls fairly gleamed. Vera, Mazie, and Frances stood serving drinks from behind the bar. Vanessa and Mozart stood across from Vera, Kaspar and Hushour across from

Frances. Swede, Ben, and the banker stood apart with drinks in their hands. They were talking among themselves. John Schutte and three men Fargo didn't recognize sat at one of the poker tables. All were laughing about something. A man stood looking out a front window. He held a rifle. Mazie and the three women leaned on the far end of the bar. All had glasses before them. Mazie was undoubtedly hearing their nightmares. Reverend Orr's face was already mashed to the top of a poker table. One of his outstretched hands gripped an empty whiskey bottle. Fargo presumed the preacher guzzled it dry in one tilt.

Fargo stepped to the near end of the bar and rested his left foot on the brass rail.

Frances yelped, "Fargo! Good to see you!" She hurried to him and poured a glass full with bourbon.

Conversation ceased as faces turned toward him.

He moved to the middle of the bar and told the women and saloon girls to gather 'round so he wouldn't have to shout. When they obeyed, he said, "First things first, ladies. There's six of you and four rooms, which means some doubling up. Also, Mazie, you and Vera and Frances see if you can find some bedclothes for these women. Tomorrow, I'll give you the money and you three can take them shopping for new clothes and shoes, whatever else it is you females wear. I know they're dog-tired, so why don't you take them upstairs now and sort out who sleeps where?"

Ouida snapped, "I want a room all by myself."

Frances snorted, "Lady, you got it. We wouldn't have it any other way."

Fargo watched them move up the stairs, then looked at Hushour and Kaspar. "Everyone here?"

"Avery Pearson said he'd bring two others," Kaspar answered. "They'll be long any minute now."

Vanessa went behind the bar and refilled their glasses. Pouring Fargo a fresh drink, she said, "Mozart and I heard you run out the back door. What happened?"

"The piano man—"

"Carl Simpson?" blurted Ben Voss.

"Yes. He was standing out in the hallway, listening to

our conversation." He glanced at Vanessa and grinned. "I'll pay you for all those two-by-fours I broke trying to get out of that framework. Simpson got away. Rode west on Dynamite Street."

"You should have shot the skinny bastard," Vanessa replied. "Good riddance, though. You don't owe me anything."

Three men wearing gun belts pushed through the swinging doors. One towered taller than the other two. He was well-dressed and had a matched pair of navy Colts in his holsters. The other two had Smith & Wessons like Kid. The taller man joined Hushour and Kaspar, who made the introductions. "Avery, you and Sam and Josh meet Skye Fargo, the Trailsman."

The shorter two nodded.

Avery Pearson said, "Glad to know you, Fargo. Neil says trouble's brewing."

"Big trouble." Fargo glanced as Kaspar. "Is everybody here who's coming? I don't want to say this but once."

Kaspar nodded. "When you reckon it will come?" he asked, his grizzly face all squinched, as if to make it appear as fearsome as possible.

"Can't predict when, only that it will happen. They could ride in any minute, or it might be tomorrow or the next day. But they will ride in. You can count on it."

"How many?" Eldon Crabtree asked.

"I'm not sure. There were twenty to start with. I—"

"Twenty?" the old man croaked, and the squinch fell away. He glanced among the faces and added, "You killed some, didn't you?"

"Oh, yes. Three that I know."

"Goddamn, seventeen's still a whole lot," the old man persisted. Nodding furiously, he asked hopefully, "You got some more, though, ain't that right, son?"

"Probably. It was storming and at night. I was more concerned about getting those women out of there than anything else. Yes, I shot or blew up some more. There's no telling how many are too wounded to ride. I'd guess we can expect ten, maybe twelve. Certainly no less than eight."

"Eight's a bunch," Pearson muttered. Several heads bobbed agreement.

Ben Voss found his voice. "From which direction do you think they will hit us?"

"Hard to say, Ben. West seems most likely, but the man leading them, Russell Bomar, is a crafty devil. If it was me, I'd split them and come in from more than one way, especially if I had enough to divide into groups. I'm warning all of you these are desperate men. Don't think otherwise. They won't be easy. They've been together long enough for Bomar to know what he can expect from each man. Hell, they have no place to go and nothing to do but kill. They intend to take over your town, and they will die to get it. That's a promise." He looked at Vanessa. "You're at the top of Bomar's death list."

Vanessa nodded grimly. "I know, I know."

Fargo said to them, "When you leave, warn everyone, especially those living west and north of town, to load every weapon they have, lock and bar all doors and windows, then blow out all lamps. If I were them, I wouldn't sleep a wink until this is over."

Crabtree made a statement, not a question out of it when he said, "You have a plan."

"I've thought of one," Fargo replied. "You men might have a better one, though."

"No, let's hear yours," one of the men suggested. Again, heads bobbed.

Fargo counted the men before he began. "Counting me, there's twelve of us to defend Walsenburg. If we're lucky, that's even odds. The worst thing is for us to thin out our firepower, meaning it wouldn't do to set up blockades in four or more directions. If, say, Bomar's full force comes from the west, three of us couldn't stop them."

"So?" Kaspar gulped.

"So we set up barricades to fight from behind. One across Dynamite between the wagon-repair shop and the corral. Another one north on Main Street between the general store and mining office. Station four men at the west, four in the north. We can't leave our backs exposed, though. So, put one man in the church east of town on Dynamite Street and two south on Main. I'll be outside the bank and rush to help the group who needs me most. Then we set up a third in the center of the intersection. If either group has to fall back, they can go there. If it gets too hot in the intersection, there's nothing left but to go south and split up to fight from the hotel and here in the saloon."

"Sounds as good as any," Josh offered.

Mozart broke his silence. "You didn't count me in."

Fargo looked at Mozart's hard stare. Clearly the man was offended. Fargo had the answer ready. "I was coming to you. Mozart, you get the toughest job of all—protecting all these women. You heard me say the men will die in the effort to get at Vanessa. You know Russell Bomar?"

"I do. The man's not human."

"Then kill him the instant he busts in."

"I will. If he is the only one I manage to kill, it will be Russell Bomar."

"All right, men, I guess that's it," Fargo said. "Neil, how about you and Fred being in charge of setting up the barricades? I'm bushed."

"Be glad to," Fred volunteered for Kaspar.

Pearson said, "Anybody needs ammunition, come over to my place. Pearson Firearms is breaking its cash on the barrel-head policy. Ammo's free tonight."

Fargo watched them walk out, several patting Avery's back.

Vanessa and Fargo drank without speaking while watching Mozart nail three big planks across the inside of the back door and test his work for security. Satisfied, Mozart came back in the saloon, positioned a chair in the corner next to the alcove, then blew out the lamps. After dousing the last one, he sat and leaned the back of the chair against the corner. Fargo heard him cock a revolver. Mozart was alert and ready for trouble to come through the front door.

The saloon was silent. Not one sound came from upstairs. Vanessa and Fargo saw only their own dark forms from where they stood across the bar from each other. Their hands met on the bartop. She squeezed his and held the grip while they walked the length of the bar and into her room across from the office. Inside, she lit a lamp, then raised onto her toes and tilted her face and open mouth to his.

Vanessa's arms wrapped around Fargo and she embraced him tightly. They kissed openmouthed. She mewed. Her passion had a short fuse. He felt her breathing quicken, her hot breaths and hotter tongue mate with and encircle his. He slid both hands down her arched back, filled them with her quivering buttock cheeks, and lifted her off the floor. Her fingernails dug into his back, signaling an inner explosion of sexual giving and receiving was about to occur.

Panting, she broke the wet kiss and looked deeply, ravenously into his lake-blue eyes. Her hands moved to frame his face. She kissed him again, more hungrily than before. He drew her Venus mound to his crotch. She responded and rubbed them to full fury with slow movements of her hips.

Gasping hotly, she murmured, "I'm ready. Oh, Jesus, am I ever."

He lowered and released her. Vanessa's fingers darted to his shirt and Levi's and expertly started undoing the buttons. He removed the gun belt and put it in a sofa chair, then tossed his hat toward a corner and pulled his shirt off.

With the removal of the gun belt, the widow squatted, drew the Levi's and shorts down, and curled her fingers around his hard staff. He felt her hot lips meet the swollen summit, her tongue caress the crown, the tip swirl through the slit on it, then search below the head when she took it and more between her moist lips.

He took her head in his hands and coaxed her to take it all. She eagerly complied, rotating her head to work him deeply inside, where the hot, soft tissue of her throat sent his passion to new heights. His throbbing foretold a premature eruption he didn't want. He moved her head back, felt the slow, reluctant withdrawal. Her lips smacked with the release. She rose smiling and with her happy eyes locked on his.

Fargo sat on the edge of her wide four-poster bed and pulled off his boots, socks, and Levi's. She stepped between his legs and held him by the face again. Her eyes were filled with excited anticipation. He unbuttoned her blouse and drew it apart. A pair of voluptuous breasts stood out like honeydew melons cut in half. Fargo believed they would taste just as sweet. The erect brownish-pink nipples stabbed out from soft-tan areolae the size of quarters. His mouth engulfed the left breast first.

She tilted her head back, mashed the pillowy mound hard to him, and cried, "Harder . . . suck hard. Bite me . . . oh, Jesus, yes, bite me."

He raked the nipple and areola with his tongue, then rolled the nipple between his teeth. Vanessa screamed, "That's it . . . more . . . don't stop. Yes, yes!"

He moved to the right breast and filled his mouth with it. She gasped, "Wonderful . . . I'm on fire, burning up." She started swaying her bosom across his wet lips. The sensation wasn't enough for the hot-blooded woman. She clutched his head and moved it in the opposite direction, doubling the enjoyment. She gasped loudly, "Please, Fargo . . . oh, God . . . oh, God, how wonderful!"

Continuing to suck on the heaving breasts, he pulled her skirt down. She drew back from him. Her glistening areolae and nipples stood majestically, fulfilled, before his eyes. She kicked the skirt away, took off her shoes, and backed halfway to the door.

She began by turning her back to him. Fargo propped on his elbows and looked at her fine ass. The roundness, an inverted heart's shape, of the milk-white cheeks rolled in smoothly to form a most alluring crack that in turn opened slightly at the bottom and defined and emphasized the graceful rolling under of the perfectly symmetrical cheeks. Looking over her shoulder at him, she tensed the cheeks muscles. Dimples appeared on both. She relaxed them; then, controlling the muscles of either cheek, she bobbed first one then the other cheek for him.

She parted her legs, bent forward, and touched her toes. Her long auburn hair swept on the floor. She looked at him from between her hanging breasts. He studied the fluff of auburn hair bulging from the bottom of her crack. A middle finger appeared below the fluff and felt inside it. The moist finger shone when withdrawn. She raised and slowly turned to face him, her hands cupping her breasts. She dipped her chin to touch her breastbone and drew her right knee to her belly. A flick of her head and the auburn hair fell to cover the left side of her pretty face. She smiled wickedly. The sultry pose aroused Fargo anew. He beckoned her to him.

She came slowly, her lips pursed impishly, and knelt beside him on the bed. "Your way or mine, big man?"

"Surprise me."

"I want to watch your face, run my fingers over your beautiful body."

"Be my guest."

"But first, we have to get everything good and slippery."

"But of course."

He moved to the far side of the bed. Vanessa reclined in its center. In one movement he rolled onto hands and knees, his hard member dragging in her cleavage and the fluff inches from his lips. She massaged her breasts with the crest before consuming it in her mouth. She relished anew his length while he tasted of her genital charms, which he found both swollen with passionate anticipation and most savory. She moaned, "My brain is swirling. I've never seen such beauty. Uhmm, you taste so good."

He parted the opening and probed deeply with his salivating tongue. She writhed, squealing, "Oh, God . . . yes, yes . . . oh, God, yes." He felt the trembling of her silky smooth thighs when she clamped them to his cheeks.

With him leading, they rolled over, their faces buried on each other's enchantment. She rose and swiveled to straddle and face him. Her chest heaved uncontrollably and her flared eyes flashed with a wild excitement he'd never seen before. Vanessa's hips raised. She reached behind her and grasped him. He felt his throbbing member rub down her crack and the blood-swollen crest part the opening and be placed for entry. He gripped the curves of her hips.

As if by a shouted command, she squatted and he shoved simultaneously. As her head lolled, she screamed, "Aaayeeeiii! Aaayeeeiii!" He pulled down on her hips and thrust his upward. She gulped twice and gasped, "Yes, oh, yes, yes."

He set her hips to swaying and made his pendulate against the motion. "Aaaah," she screamed, and included a rocking, fanning movement between the wide swings of her hips.

"Yes, yes, yes," she moaned. "More, I want more . . . all of it . . . harder, please, faster . . . oh, God, go faster, deeper. Oh, Jesus, I think I can take it all. Give it to me, please."

Her tight contraction seized his full length. He didn't think it would let go if he tried to pull out. He slammed upward and welded her soft inner tissue of the lips to his base. She moaned through gritted teeth and fell forward onto his muscled chest. Her head swung side to side. "Oh, my God," she whimpered. "Oh, my God . . . this feels wonderful . . . so good."

He felt his scrotum tightening in prelude to his gushing. It came with blinding speed, hot and uninterrupted. It went deep, and she screamed, "Aaaaghh!" A new contraction gripped his pulsing member. It squeezed and relaxed, squeezed and milked till the last drop.

Exhausted, Vanessa's body fell limp. She inhaled slowly, deeply, then emptied her lungs quickly. Fargo twisted, cupped a hand at the mouth of the flue, and blew out the lamp.

Lightning, still far in the west, winked pale flashes on the drapes covering the bedroom window. Rain started pattering on the windowpane. It meant only one thing: the storm had hurdled the Sangre de Cristos and its brunt would soon blast into Walsenburg.

He put Vanessa's head in the crook of his shoulder and stroked her back.

She nuzzled his neck and throat, whispering, "I didn't know it could feel that wonderful . . . I never knew until now. All those other men and—"

He put a finger to her lips to hush her. "Vanessa, the feeling was there all the time. Tonight you let go and found it. Now that you know it's there, you can call it up anytime."

"I don't know that I ever will want it again . . . except when I'm with you, my love." She sighed softly and snuggled more comfortably to him.

Content to be in each other's arms, they lay still and quiet and listened to the wind and rain strengthen. Sleep came swift and easy.

11

A sound other than rumbling thunder tore through the shrieking wind and beating rain. Fargo's eyes opened instantly. He eased Vanessa off him and swung his feet to the floor. The drapes offered precious little veiling of the brilliant lightning flashes.

Vanessa stirred awake while he was pulling on his shirt. "What is it?" she asked sleepily. "Come back to bed."

Before he could answer, a rapping on the door turned his head. Mozart said, "They're coming."

"I heard the roar. A buffalo rifle. I'm dressing now. I'll be out in a minute."

He pulled on his drawers and Levi's. Sitting to draw on the socks and boots, he answered her. "Get up and dress. Mozart took care of the back door, but not this window. Go in the office and lock the door behind you. Don't open it for anyone but me or Mozart." Lightning cracked. He glanced to her clock next to the lamp on the night table. "It's midnight. With luck this will be over quick and we can still get a night's rest."

She left the bed as he buckled on the gun belt. "This is insane—grown men fighting in a storm."

"Makes sense," Fargo told her. "Bomar knows what he's doing." He paused long enough to hug and kiss her, then hurried from the bedroom.

Mozart stood in the corner by the alcove. Orr, oblivious to the storm raging outside, looked as if he hadn't moved an inch since Fargo last saw him. A boom of thunder accompanied by blasts of lightning shook the building, rattled the front windows. Mozart and Fargo exchanged nods. Snugging his hat down, Fargo hurried outside.

Rounding the corner at a dead run, he sloshed through

the muddy water coursing down Dynamite Street and went to the wagons Kaspar and others had turned over and now stood behind facing west. The barricade connected the wagon-repair shop and corral. A stack of barrels filled the gap between the end of one wagon and the corral fencing. Kaspar wasn't giving them one inch to squeeze through.

Fargo came up behind him. "Seen them yet?"

Neil squinted into the driving rain as he answered, "No, but they're out there, all right. Anderson don't shoot that damn Hawken in the middle of the night for no reason at all. The way we figure it, they're looking at us, making up their minds."

Voss, Crabtree, and a man Fargo hadn't met also manned the blockade. All three were armed with rifles and revolvers. Kaspar held a .52 Spencer.

"Keep your eyes open, men. Expect the unexpected. I'll go see what's happening up Main." Fargo wheeled and ran next to the repair business and Crabtree's darkened bank to the corner. Lightning flashed. Thunder boomed.

Four overturned Studebaker farm wagons formed a box in the middle of the intersection. Two other overturned wagons blocked Main Street in the north between the Schuttes' place and Doc Williamson's office building. Fargo rushed up the middle of the street and to the barrier manned by Schutte, Hushour, Swede, and another man.

Schutte left his rifle pointing north over the side of a wagon when he half-turned to greet Fargo. "Sorry to pull you out of a warm bed, Mr. Fargo, but it looks like they prefer a night battle."

The rain was coming down in bucketsful. "And a wet one at that," Fargo added. "Seen any movement, any sign they're out there?"

"None," Hushour replied. "But what with this blasted rain and all, they could walk right in and be on us before we know it."

What Fred Hushour said was true. During daylight it would be damn difficult to see thirty feet into this heavy downpour, Fargo thought. He glanced back of him. Not one light burned in any of the structures.

As he watched, it seemed that a bolt of lightning struck one of the wagons comprising the box. It exploded and hurled the other three in as many directions. For an instant the intersection, bank, feed store across from it, the hotel, and the barbershop were bathed in the garish light. On the heels of the blast came another, this one near the western barrier.

"This is it," Fargo shouted. He ran back to the corner and looked around the corner of the bank.

As he predicted only moments earlier, the unexpected had happened. Bomar and his men were using dynamite. The barricade lay in shambles, Kaspar and the others sprawled in the muddy street. The blast had also taken out most of the corral fencing on the street side. Panicked horses streamed onto the street, whinnying their fright. Five horsemen, all leaning over their mounts' necks, were charging in.

Before Fargo could fire a round, another dynamite blast jolted him against the bank's front door. He braced a hand on it and looked up Main. The stick had dropped short of the wagons, but close enough to topple them. Swede and the others had their shoulders on the wagon beds, shoving the wagons back on their sides. Six of Bomar's men were charging in, firing rapidly. Fargo ran to help those at the north blockade.

Swede and the others were returning fire by the time Fargo ran up and added his gun. Four of the attackers broke out of the pack. One reined sharp left and headed for a house north and east of the jail. Two swerved off Main and rode behind the jail. One left Main on the right and disappeared behind Doc Williamson's office. Fargo swung the Colt to catch him when he passed the open space between Williamson's and the structure occupied by Erskine Mining Company. For an instant the rider was caught in a flash of the unceasing lightning. Fargo squeezed the trigger. The Colt barked. The rider fell from the saddle and tumbled on the muddy ground.

Swede ran alongside the wagons to the opening that separated the Schuttes' place and the general store. Fargo saw him raise his revolver and fire twice. Swede yelled back, "Got one! The other made it!"

A terrible explosion rocked Walsenburg. It knocked Fargo and the others to the ground and halted the charging riders dead in their tracks. Fargo looked up to see the roof on Pearson Firearms splintering apart as it went sky-high. The walls simply disintegrated as the fiery mushroom blasted up and outward.

No sooner did the Pearson building blow up than the ground shook again. The feed store on the corner erupted in flames.

An instant later another blast of dynamite shook the buildings and ground, this one from behind the hotel.

Fargo shouted for everybody to fall back to the intersection. They ran, firing at the two riders still on Main Street. To Fargo's surprise, Voss and Crabtree had managed to get up and retreat to the intersection. Both were wounded: Voss's left upper shirt sleeve was bloody, Crabtree clutched his right shoulder. Fargo hunkered with them behind one of the all but destroyed wagons. He glanced among the remains of the other wagons and saw Schutte, Swede, and Hushour. Schutte's blood mingled with rainwater on his left thigh.

Pearson's gun and that of the other man stationed south on Main fired. Fargo glanced that way. Two of the men from Saint Lucifer ran from between the smithy's shop and the ruins of Pearson's business. As they came onto Main, Pearson stepped out of the smithy's place and challenged them. Shots were exchanged. Pearson slumped into the mud. Both men spun and fired at the other defender, aiming at them from around the corner of the land-office building. Fargo saw the man double over and fall forward.

The outlaws headed for the saloon. Fargo tensed to spring and take them on, then settled back down when he heard a Smith & Wesson firing from beyond them. At first he thought Pearson was firing, then he saw Kid Ballas riding in. Both of Bomar's butchers were knocked off the ground by Kid's bullets. Kid dismounted in front of the saloon and ran to Fargo.

They exchanged the deadly grins while firing at allusive targets. "How many?" Kid asked.

"Not as many as before," Fargo replied.

"Did you find her?" Kid asked.

"She's in the Buckhorn," Fargo answered, then added, "I'm concerned about those other women in the saloon."

"I'll go take care of them," Kid replied.

"Do that," Fargo agreed.

Kid Ballas ran, firing from a crouch, to the saloon.

Fargo spun and shot a man on foot coming at him from the north. After he shot, he heard the Sharps fire from an upstairs window in the hotel. He glanced over his shoulder and saw Elmo standing not two paces away with a dagger in his upraised hand, a startled expression on his face, and a blossoming splotch of red on his shirt front.

Elmo toppled backward, dead before he splattered into the mud. Fargo's eyes kicked up to the window. Becky lowered the butt of the smoking Sharps from her shoulder. Jennie stood behind her.

An outlaw ran from behind the burning feed store onto Dynamite Street. Hushour swung his revolver on him and fired. The raider catapulted backward.

For a moment, all firing ceased. Lightning flashed. Thunder rumbled through the stricken town. Fargo's gaze swept the blazing firelit streets in all four directions. Fire from the feed store had leapt to the general store, which now burned. Pearson Firearms was an inferno, and its blaze had caught the café next to it on fire, as it had this end of the smithy's shop.

Fargo felt uneasy that he hadn't glimpsed Russell Bomar or his henchman, Frank Selman. He cut his eyes back to the saloon and told Hushour, "Keep everyone here. This isn't over yet."

As he spoke, an outlaw raced from behind the bank and across Dynamite Street to the barbershop. Two others darted out the door and joined him on the porch. Volleys of fire were exchanged as the trio hurried to the saloon.

As they came in front of it, Carl Simpson streaked from his hiding place between the Buckhorn and the café, crossed the muddy street, and joined up with them.

To Fargo's surprise, Neil Kaspar had somehow made it to the swinging doors during all the exploding and gunplay. The old man lay balled up on the porch at the entrance. He still gripped his weapon.

Fargo ran toward the saloon. He dropped one of the foursome near the double doors. The man bringing up the rear dived through a window opening, its glass, like most all others in town, blown inside by the explosion at Pearson Firearms. One of the others, followed by Simpson, leapt over Kaspar and rushed inside before Fargo could swing the Colt on them. Kaspar raised the Spencer and fired. The shot rang out with several others fired inside the saloon.

Fargo rushed through the double doors and halted to wait for a flash of lightning to show him the state of affairs.

A monstrous cracking, not unlike a giant ripping sheet of canvas ten feet thick, split the heavens. The bolt of lightning that struck and exploded behind the saloon shook and rattled it violently. Through the din, Fargo heard the back door crash inward. Lightning flashed. He saw Mozart standing in the corner by the alcove, Orr slumped over the table, and Kid on the top landing of the stairs. Frank Selman ran out of the downstairs hallway, fired at but missed Fargo, and moved for the stairs. A single bullet from Kid's Smith & Wesson tore a hunk out of Selman's head.

Bomar hurtled through the open hallway door and lunged shoulder-first onto the office door. It and he fell inside. Vanessa shrieked. Firelight spilled out into the hallway. Fargo ran to it. So did Kid Ballas and Mozart.

Fargo swung around the splintered doorjamb and inside the office. Russell and Vanessa stood behind the desk. Russell held her head back by the hair entwined in his fist, her exposed throat about to be cut by the long knife he held in the other.

Fargo dived over the desk and grabbed the knife hand in the nick of time. All three fell onto the floor. Vanessa struggled free, rose, and ran to Kid, who stood just inside the doorway. He clutched her close to him. Mozart stood in the doorway. Their eyes stayed on the two big men locked in a death struggle on the floor.

Each held the other's throat in one hand and the wrist

of the choking hand gripped in the other, straining to pull it free. They tumbled, wrestling each other for an advantage, with legs locked. Russell released his hold on Fargo's wrist and moved the hand next to the one choking Fargo.

It was the only mistake Bomar made.

Fargo used the free hand to lever Russell over to the blazing fireplace. He grabbed the man's half-head of hair, twisted his fingers in it, and slowly edged the good side of Russell's head toward the leering fiery devil's head.

Russell, clearly feeling the fire, found a reserve of strength and increased the pressure of his stranglehold. Fargo's hearing started to buzz and starry flashes swirled in his blurred vision. Life was draining away.

Kid moved Vanessa out of his way and raised his gun to aim at Bomar's head.

"No," Fargo grunted to him.

Reluctantly, Kid lowered the Smith & Wesson.

Fargo's fingers, enmeshed in Russell's hair, inched the man's face into the blaze. Fargo willed himself not to let go, but to continue.

Bomar's will cracked. He let go of Fargo's throat to attack the hand bringing him fiery pain.

In that instant Fargo pushed the good side of Russell's face onto the burning devil's head. Russell screamed. Fargo fused the screaming man's face to the devil's head. Hair burned, searing flesh sizzled and began melting.

Bomar went limp under Fargo's grasp. He pulled Bomar away from the devil's head, leaving a strip of spitting flesh to shrivel and char.

He reached to his calf and withdrew his throwing knife. Baring the unconscious man's throat, he slashed it and ended Russell Bomar's misery . . . and God only knew how many others.

The Trailsman wiped the blade on the dead man's shirt, returned the knife to its sheath, and rose. The grandfather clock chimed. Fargo glanced at it. The time was half-past-twelve.

It was over.

12

Fargo, Mozart, and Kid Ballas, who held Vanessa close, went into the dark saloon. The pungent smell of gunsmoke hung heavy in the room.

Neil Kaspar groaned. Fargo and Kid went to him and helped the old man inside. They sat him in a chair at the nearest poker table. Kaspar groaned he was okay, "But I can't hear or see a damn thing," he complained.

Fargo recognized the symptoms. The old man was in shock from the blast of dynamite. It affected his inner ears, which in turn affected his equilibrium. That's why the old man couldn't stand. The scrapes on his face looked bad, but weren't anything to be concerned about. "Sit there for a while, Pops. It'll all come back shortly." He glanced to Kid and asked, "Mind getting Doc to check him out? Tell him there's others to tend to."

Kid nodded and hurried out into the stormy night.

Mozart started lighting lamps. Vanessa stepped behind the bar and started pouring drinks.

In addition to Selman's twisted body near the foot of the stairs, three others littered the room: one just inside the window he leapt through, another on the floor between the bar and a poker table, and Carl Simpson lying on his stomach half on and half off the bar.

The six women were huddled on the walkway at the top landing, staring down on the grizzly scene. Reverend Orr still sat with his upper body slumped over the poker table.

Mozart explained. "Kid got the one by the window and that one by the stairs. When lightning flashed, I caught the one running next to the bar. That other one ran in and dived over the bar. The old man shot him in midair."

Fargo joined Mozart at the bar and they drank with Vanessa while waiting for Doc and Kid to come. Instead, the walking wounded started filing through the double doors, Schutte in the lead. Blood showed high on his left pant leg. Favoring the leg, he limped to the bar. Ben Voss followed him. Voss had been shot in the left upper arm. Eldon Crabtree sauntered in with a splotch of blood on his shirt at the right shoulder. As he came to the bar, he shook his head and grinned sheepishly, as though it was his fault for getting shot. Behind him came an unwounded man, who had guarded the east from the church and didn't fire one shot. Vanessa poured all of them a drink.

After a few minutes Kid and Doc brought Avery Pearson inside and sat him at the table with Neil Kaspar. Pearson's head was a bloody mess. Kid explained, "He was staggering in the street down by the smithy's."

Doc placed his black medical satchel on the table and said, "Avery's not near as bad off as he looks. Got a crease in his scalp. While it'll bleed like hell, he won't bleed to death. Hear that, Avery? Said you aren't going to die." Avery barely nodded. Doc started wiping the blood away.

Those at the bar reported three defenders Fargo didn't know had been killed.

Doc announced, "Kid found me at Millie Wilson's cabin tending to that woman who isn't pregnant anymore. All those explosions brought her baby early. Mother and daughter are doing fine, thank you. Somebody, I could use a hard drink." He glanced at the preacher and added, "But not what you poured down Orr."

While Doc continued to administer to the wounded, Fargo, Mozart, Kid, and the other nonwounded men dragged the corpses out in the muddy street. "We'll get the rest of their dead the next time the sun shines," Fargo told them.

Everybody was quickly patched up. Doc told them to go home and get some rest, that he'd see them in his office later in the day. He followed them outside.

Kid asked Fargo, "What did you run into at Camp Saint Lucifer?"

"Rain, mud—a storm much like this one—and twenty of the devil's worst. Now, Kid, you're going to describe Jennie Hollis to me."

"I thought you said she was in the hotel?"

"That's correct, but I still want you to tell me about her."

Kid held a hand out between his chest and shoulders. "She's about this tall."

"Go on," Fargo replied, now knowing she wasn't the rancher's daughter unless she grew mighty damn fast in two month's time.

"Jennie's thirteen and—"

Fargo held his hand up to stop Kid. "Say no more. The blonde over in the hotel isn't her. I don't know who the hell she is, but she's not Jennie Hollis."

"Then who is? What happened to Mr. and Mrs. Hollis' girl?"

"Damn good question, Kid. I'm going to find out." Fargo took another swig of bourbon and headed for the swinging doors.

He breezed through the dark lobby and up the stairs to door Number 9. He found it unlocked and stepped inside. The lamp on the night table burned. Jennie lay wide awake on the bed with the covers drawn over her bosom and her hair splayed on the pillow. It was obvious to him that she expected his entrance. She looked at him and smiled.

The smile wavered when he said nothing while shucking his clothes right where he stood just inside the door. Fargo's stare stayed drilled on her eyes all the time. Her gaze lowered to his groin as he pulled off the Levi's and underdrawers, and he saw her catch a breath.

He stepped to the bed, flung back the covers. With her eyes widened and her legs full open Jennie breathed heavily, excitedly.

Fargo mounted the blonde. Her legs came up, raising her hips off the bed and positioning the eager opening for him to enter. His summit touched her V. He felt her ankles lock behind his neck and her fingers dig into his hard buttock cheeks. They moved in unison, him thrusting hard, her hips rising equally as fast and mightily. He went all the way in the hot, velvety sheath. She screamed joyously and gasped loudly, "Oh! Oh! More . . . more!"

She levered her hips up to help force the penetration deeper and began gyrating them, moaning her euphoria.

"Faster, please go faster . . . rub hard on the top of mine. Oh, Jesus, yes . . . yes, yes . . . that's it, that's it. Aaaggh!"

He rotated to widen and massage the tender membrane of her slick nook, to increase her pleasure, which already trembled through her body. She gulped, then gasped, "Oh! Oh! That's it. Don't stop. Please, don't stop."

He pulled her legs down. She locked the ankles on the small of his back. He took her left nipple, areola, and the heaving breast below them in his mouth and swirled her a new bliss. Jennie cried her ecstasy, "Suck harder, Fargo! Bite me! Oh, God! Yes, yes, yes! Wonderful . . . I can't believe this is happening to me. Oh, God, I'm com—"

A bolt of lightning struck, its explosion concurrent with theirs. Thunder rumbled the length of Dynamite Street, shook the rain-drenched town and the sweat-covered lovers.

Jennie murmured, "I don't want it to end. Please, make it go on forever. I didn't know it could be like this . . . so glorious, so fulfilling."

He slowed the pounding pace and changed the rhythm to a gentle hip swing, which she met. Her ankles unlocked and for a moment her knees rubbed in opposite directions on his sides, then clung to them when her heels dug into his buttocks. She raised her open mouth to his and kissed him tenderly while embracing tightly. Slowly, her legs lowered, but did not part. She crossed them to keep him captive a moment longer and flexed her groin muscles to make him feel her great pleasure.

He rolled her to lie on top of him and kissed her fervently. Finally, he asked, "Who are you?"

"I lied to you. My real name is Jennie, okay, only the last name is McIntyre."

"What happened to Jennie Hollis?"

"Jake Feemster and Billy Suddeth brought the poor little girl to the camp. She was only thirteen. I befriended her. She told me about Kid. That's how I knew Kid Ballas' name."

"What happened to her. Is she dead?"

"Yes," Jennie answered softly. "Let's say Jennie Hollis died of pneumonia and let it go at that."

Fargo knew that wasn't the reason, but accepted it. He nodded grimly.

She looked into his eyes and said, "Oh, Fargo, I too wish it hadn't happened, but it did, and there's no bringing her back. Life has to go on." Embracing him, she whispered, "Mine and yours."

Of course she's right, he told himself. He raised a hand to her chin and tilted her face up and kissed her. Jennie's hug tightened and she sighed, as though a pure white curtain had finally been drawn to block out the bad memories of her recent past and form the backdrop of a new chapter in her life.

Fargo awakened first. Bright morning sunrays spilled through the upstairs bedroom window and onto the sleeping pretty face lying in the crook of his left shoulder. He yawned and the scant movement was enough to open Jennie's eyes. Her fingers traced circles on his right pectoral muscle, then teased on the nipple. She mewed sleepily, "You were right, Fargo. I will never forget last night."

He smiled. "I hate to say this, but now it's time to complete my business and be on my way. Get dressed and we'll go to the saloon."

"So soon? Can't it wait?" She moved to hold him down.

Patting her ass, he chuckled. "Jennie McIntyre, if he let you, you'd wear a man out in short order. I'll be two days getting my strength back." He drew the cover down and swung his feet to the floor.

She yawned, stretched, and pulled the covers back over her. Watching him dress, she said, "You're not the only one who's wore out. I'd thought after riding bareback for a week nothing could make me sore down there, but I admit I was wrong. You go on. I'll be along shortly . . . if I can stand and walk."

He bent and kissed her before leaving.

Freida blanched when she saw him come down the stairs and pass through the lobby.

Fargo touched the brim of his hat. " 'Morning, ma'am. How's Ben feeling today?"

"Sore. He's at the saloon. Most everybody is." She glanced to the stairs, obviously expecting to see Jennie on them.

Crossing the street, Fargo counted thirteen bodies lying in a row in the mud outside the saloon.

He paused outside the double doors to see who was inside. As Freida had stated, quite a number were, and all of last night's defenders.

Kid and Vanessa were holding hands. She was looking up at his face as though in a trance she didn't want to come out of; the sparkle Fargo had seen in her eyes when she looked at Kid that first time seemed to twinkle with a newfound satisfaction. Kid looked like he hadn't had a wink's sleep all night.

Millie and the three saloon girls busied themselves behind the bar, on which sat four pots of delicious-smelling fresh coffee. Apparently Millie brewed the coffee especially for this occasion, for those who didn't partake of stronger libations before high noon.

Orr remained slumped over the poker table. Mozart stood at the far end of the bar looking at the men lined up at it with one of their boots on the brass rail. All of the women from Camp Saint Lucifer except Jennie and Nancy sat at a poker table. They held drinks or coffee mugs, looked rested and clean.

Fargo pushed inside and went to stand at the bar between Doc and Kaspar, who looked fit as a fiddle.

Millie smiled, "Coffee, bourbon, or me?"

"Let's start with coffee."

She obliged.

Fargo pulled the envelope from his hip pocket and handed it to Kid. "Jennie Hollis died of pneumonia. Explain to your boss I can't accept this money because I couldn't deliver his daughter."

Kid nodded and handed back the envelope. "Mr. Hollis told me to tell you to keep it no matter what. They just want to know what happened to her, whether she's dead or alive."

Fargo understood. He pocketed the envelope and looked at the women at the poker table. "You ladies decided what to do?"

Ouida answered first. "I'm going back home to Indiana, where life is simple. I've seen all the West I want to see."

Jennie walked inside just in time to see Becky inspect her fingers and hear her say solemnly, "I hope to go to Grand Junction. That's where we were going when I got captured." She started crying and sniffled, "I hope Vincent will have me. I love him so much, really I do, but I'm so ashamed."

Jennie took her in her arms and held her tight. "Go ahead and bawl it out, Becky. He'll take you back. Wait and see. You couldn't help what happened. None of us could."

"Yeah," Claudine said, "make up a story. Don't tell him or anybody else what happened. All he will know is what you tell him."

Fargo looked at Claudine. She shrugged and said, "I don't know. Maybe I'll stay here in Walsenburg till these nightmares go away and I get my mind back. I don't have anyplace to go."

"Yes, you do," Malva Schutte said as she came to hold Claudine's hands. "John and I have plenty of spare room. You can live with us."

Both women started crying.

Loudon cleared her throat and offered, "No man will have me. Not after my being the Utes' captive all that time. Certainly not after being a love slave in Camp Saint Lucifer." She looked at Vanessa, held in Kid's arms. "Me and Frances talked last night. If there's one thing I do know how to do, it's screwing. I'd like to work here, if you'll have me."

Vanessa nodded.

Jennie said, "Mrs. Voss visited me last night before all hell broke loose. We talked. She's the new school superintendent. I told her I finished school. She offered me a teaching position and said I could help out at the Buckhorn during summer vacation. I took her up on it."

Vanessa led Kid and Mozart out to the middle of the room. John Schutte stepped forward and handed her something, then moved aside.

Vanessa said, "Folks, I have an announcement to

make—actually, a proclamation. As of today, Kid Ballas is the new sheriff of Walsenburg." She pinned the sheriff's badge to his shirt and kissed him on the mouth. Kid's face turned beet-red. She held him back and sighed, "Well, you will just have to get accustomed to it, Kid, because from now on, you're my one and only sweetie."

She stepped in front of Mozart and looked up at him. "You have been a dear and faithful friend. I appreciate your loyalty and the protection you have given me. I now suggest you make a life of your own without worrying over me. Mozart, you are henceforth Kid Ballas' deputy." Pinning the badge on his shirt, she added, "Look after him, Mozart." He nodded; she raised on tiptoes and kissed him.

Doc asked gravely, "What are we going to do with all those outlaws you men killed?" Then he suggested an answer. "I'm for dumping the whole lot of 'em, as is, in a common grave."

Kaspar quickly added, "Unmarked, of course."

Chair legs scraped hard on the floor. Everyone turned and looked toward the raucous sound.

Reverend Orr's gangly scarecrowlike body bolted upright and stood on wobbly legs. His left palm, planted on top of the poker table, steadied him. The right arm shot straight up, the bony index finger stabbing heavenward. The preacher's big sunken eyes fairly blazed with frightful censure, as though God might be holding court from inside them and was about to hand down a terrible sentencing.

Everybody drew back a tad and held their breaths. An instantaneous silence flooded the saloon.

It was clearly the preacher who shouted, "Romans Six, Verse Twenty-three," but it could have been God who roared the scathing judgment, " 'The wages of sin is death!' " And it was definitely the preacher who added, "Hallelujah, praise the Lord. Amen!" and sank to the floor as the fire went out in his eyes.

Sprawled on the floor, Reverend Orr blubbered, "Orr One, Verse One: bartender, whiskey here." He started snoring softly.

Look for Skye Fargo's 100th adventure next month in the blockbuster supernovel: RIVERBOAT GOLD Trailsman #100

> *1860, a time when the future had already wrapped the land in its long, grim shadow and killing was as much an omen as an act . . .*

"No, you hear me? No!"

"We just thought it might be easier if we dry-gulched him before he reached the cabin, like halfway down the hill."

"You stay out of sight on top of the hill and that's all you do. This is no ordinary cowpoke. This is Skye Fargo, the Trailsman. This is a man who can outtrail the Pawnee, outfox the Comanche, and outfight the Crow. Some say he's part cougar and part hawk. You four try ambushing him anywhere near that cabin and he'll see you, hear you, smell you, or just plain feel you. While you're waiting he'll have you in his sights."

"It was a thought."

"A goddamn dumb one. You stay on top of the hill and wait. I've five men who're going to try and take him along the way. If they don't do it, then we wait till he's in the cabin with the girl. That'll be your only chance to take him, when his attention is on the girl. After you take him, you bring him to me. We know he got the letter, but we don't know how much was in it. You got it all straight now?"

"Yes, sir."

Excerpt from RIVERBOAT GOLD

"You stay hidden on top of the hill, watch the cabin for the signal, and then move in. That'll be your only chance to take him. You stick to the goddamn plan. It's been carefully worked out. Now get moving."

The man's eyebrows, thick, bushy, and black, knitted together as he watched the others hurry away. He spat in disgust.

The big man rode casually, not hurrying, sitting easily astride the magnificent Ovaro, the horse's jet-black fore- and hindquarters glistening in the sun, its pure-white midsection agleam. His lake-blue eyes scanned the terrain with deceptive casualness as he rode, and the echo of a smile edged his lips. They'd been following him all day, he was aware, through the north Iowa country southward. It was good riding country, gentle hills, mostly flat land, sparsely timbered with shadbush and slippery elm. Five riders, he'd counted. They had kept apart and stayed back, as if that was all there was to trailing someone.

Amateurs, Skye Fargo grunted. They didn't know how to follow the far side of a rock formation or move through the thick tree stands without showing their path. And they didn't know enough not to keep the same pace. They'd been easy to spot, not that they realized it. But they were cautious enough not to move closer in the open country, and so he had continued on with seeming unawareness. The day passed into the afternoon and he watched the terrain change character, grow thicker with good stands of box elder, shagbark hickory, and black walnut. He guessed that the Mississippi flowed some ten miles to his left, and he turned the pinto westward toward a long stretch of thick forest, mostly shagbark hickory. He liked hickory forests with their supply of appetizing nuts ready for the taking, with sweet insides worth fighting through the thick husks.

He sent the Ovaro into the denseness of the forest, scanned the good, thick underbrush, and glanced backward to see the five riders start to hurry forward, instantly fearful of losing their quarry. They were dependent

Excerpt from RIVERBOAT GOLD

on sight, another mark of the amateur. Fargo spotted a break in the trees and rode into it. He paused, gave them a chance to see him before he turned back into the woods. The five riders had moved in close to one another now, certain the thick forest was the place they had waited for, their chance to strike. He paused, listened, heard them closing fast, already into the forest. They were amateur trackers but probably far from amateur gunslingers, Fargo realized. His chiseled countenance tightened. It was time to give them a chance to do what they'd come to do.

He half turned the pinto and sent the horse crashing through the dense underbrush at a fast canter and heard his pursuers change direction at once to take after him. As the Ovaro crashed through the thick brush, Fargo pulled his left leg over the saddle and half jumped, half slid from the horse, his lariat in one hand. He landed on the balls of his feet and immediately sank down into the thick brush as the Ovaro raced on. Two of his pursuers came into sight almost at once, riding hard, skirting thick-trunked hickories, a third close on their heels. Fargo waited, had the lariat half raised in one hand as the last two appeared. He let the first one go by, then rose and flung the lariat as the last horsemen passed by. Fargo caught the glance of astonishment in the man's face as the noose landed around his shoulders, tightened, and yanked him from the saddle.

"Goddamn," the man cursed as he hit the ground, but Fargo was at him in three long strides. He crashed the butt of the Colt onto the man's head and the figure went limp. He'd stay that way until it was time to question him. Fargo saw the other horseman coming back toward him, alerted by his partner's curse. Fargo raised the Colt, fired, and the rider rose in the saddle before he pitched backward from his horse, a red hole in the middle of his chest.

The shot would bring the other three, Fargo knew, and he stepped back from the figure wrapped in the lariat, his eyes narrowed as he peered through the trees. The other

Excerpt from RIVERBOAT GOLD

three horsemen took only another minute to reappear, charging back toward him. He dropped to one knee, raised the Colt, and fired again. The one in the center toppled from his horse as though yanked by an invisible wire, but the other two dived headlong from their saddles and landed heavily in the brush. Fargo heard them roll and he dropped onto his stomach as a spray of bullets flew in his general direction.

He pushed backward on his stomach, found the gray-barked, thick trunk of an old hickory, and pushed himself behind it. The two men had stopped shooting, no doubt to reload. Staying behind the wide, thick trunk, Fargo raised his voice. "Talk and you can walk," he called out. "Who sent you after me?" The answer, not unexpected, sent wood chips flying from the tree as another volley of shots exploded. Fargo grimaced yet stayed put. The gunfire ended and he called out again. "You're being stupid," he said. This time a single shot answered him, the bullet hitting the other side of the thick tree trunk with a dull thud.

Fargo remained in place and he had but a few minutes to wait before he heard their whispered exchange. Another minute passed until he heard the two men begin to push their way forward through the thick underbrush. His eyes narrowed as he let his ears see for him; he stayed motionless behind the thick trunk. A grim smile touched his lips. They were doing the first smart thing they had done. They were moving toward him in unison as they spread out, obviously using a prearranged count for each move forward. He counted off to four between each rustle of the brush and smiled again. They figured to reach him at the same moment and catch him in a cross fire.

Fargo rose, holstered the big Colt, reached up, and grasped the lowest branch with both hands. He pulled himself up, swung his long legs over the branch, and sat very still for a long moment. The two men below were still moving carefully forward, one on each side of the tree. Fargo pulled himself up onto one more branch,

Excerpt from RIVERBOAT GOLD

shifted position, and drew the big Colt again. He could see the two men below, crawling on hands and knees through the brush, almost abreast of the trees. He waited, let them reach the tree, and watched as they moved around to the front of the trunk, halted, and half rose to pour a double volley of shots into the area just behind the base of the tree. He'd have been riddled, Fargo knew, had he still been there.

The two men finished their fusillades, dropped down, reloaded quickly as they waited and listened. Fargo watched as they cautiously rose. "I think we got him," one called out.

"Wrong," Fargo answered from the tree as he fired. The bullet tore into the nearest man just alongside his neck, traveled downward through his body, and came out at the front of his chest. The man shivered violently for a long moment before he collapsed to the ground. Fargo saw the other one whirl, frown up into the tree as he took desperate seconds trying to find his foe amid the branches. "Drop the gun," Fargo said, but the man followed the sound of his voice, tried bringing his gun around. Fargo fired. The shot hurtled downward into the man's upper chest and all but drove him into the ground as his legs buckled and he collapsed in an instant pool of red.

Fargo climbed from the tree, holstered the Colt, and hurried back to where he'd left the man with the lariat. He heard the man's groaned curse as he reached the spot and took hold of the rope and yanked the man to his feet. A fleshy-faced figure, the man blinked, came conscious, and stared at the big, black-haired man in front of him. "You're the only one left," Fargo said. "Talk to me."

"I don't know anything," the man muttered sullenly.

"You know who hired you," Fargo snapped.

"I wasn't there," the man said.

Fargo yanked hard on the lariat and the man sprawled forward at his feet. "I don't have time and I don't have patience," Fargo said.

Excerpt from *RIVERBOAT GOLD*

"All right, all right," the man said, and Fargo relaxed his grip on the rope. The man's fleshy face shook as he pushed to his knees. "I've got his name on a piece of paper in here," he said as he reached inside his shirt and felt around with his hand for a moment. "Here it is," he said, began to draw his hand out, and suddenly exploded with an upward lunge, a short clasp dagger with a buffalo horn grip in his hand. Fargo pulled back as the upward slash barely missed his throat, stumbled, and felt himself fall. He hit the ground and had time only to get his arms up as the man pounced at him with the short-bladed dagger upraised. Fargo managed to close his hand around the man's knife wrist, and the downward thrust of the blade stopped inches from his face. Fargo drew on the powerful muscles of his upper arms and shoulders as he slowly forced the man backward, pushed him up, and with a sudden surge of power, flipped the fleshy-faced figure away.

The man landed on his side, half rolled, and slashed out with the short dagger. Again Fargo had to jump back as the knife missed only by inches. With surprising speed the man slashed again as he dove forward and Fargo had to twist away. He didn't turn back this time, but let himself spin to the side and put more space between himself and the slashing blade. When he halted and turned, the man was charging at him again, his fleshy face twisted into a lumpy snarl. The loose end of the lariat still around his chest whipped wildly in the air as the man dived forward, the dagger raised high.

Fargo held his ground, his lips a thin line, measured split seconds, and dropped to one knee just as the flying figure reached him with the knife. He felt the blade slice the air just over his head as he dropped and lifted a tremendous blow that smashed into the man's midsection. It knocked the figure sideways in midair, and Fargo leaped up as the man hit the ground. He reached out, grasped the loose end of the lariat, yanked hard, and the man hit the ground again as he started to get up. Fargo moved quickly, sent the rope in a quick loop, and curled it

Excerpt from RIVERBOAT GOLD

around the man's neck. He let the man rise, then yanked hard on the rope, and saw the man's head swivel, his eyes virtually pop from his face. The dagger dropped from his hand as he fell to the ground, his body pointed one way, his head another. Fargo heard the hideous rattling sound that escaped the man's lips and relaxed his hold on the rope. The sound stopped and the man stared upward with eyes that would never see again.

"Stupid ass," Fargo muttered as he pulled the lariat free. He went through the man's pockets, but found nothing that revealed anything. The others offered no more. He rose, whistled and the Ovaro came through the trees toward him. He climbed onto the horse and rode south again through the trees until he emerged onto a sunlit path that led between two low hills. The attack rode with him as a shadow he couldn't shake away. Someone didn't want him to reach his destination, and the letter in his jacket pocket had suddenly taken on new dimensions. He drew to a halt at a stream that ran downhill and dismounted as the horse thirstily drank in cold, clear water.

Fargo sat down atop a half-rotted log, took the letter from his pocket, unfolded it, and began to read it once again.

Dear Skye Fargo,

I hope you remember me. It was eight years ago when I last saw you and I was only ten then. I'm writing for Captain Billy, though he didn't want me to write you. But he is in trouble. There is something very strange going on at the boat, and you were the only one I could think of who might be able to help.

Ten miles west of White Pines there are two hills next to each other. Take the one with a heavy stand of red oak. Cross to the middle and

Excerpt from RIVERBOAT GOLD

then go down to the bottom. You'll find an old cabin, I'll wait for you there. Please come.
                    Caroline Hopkins

Fargo closed the letter and returned it to his pocket. It held nothing he had missed and he found himself thinking again of Captain Billy as he rose, climbed onto the Ovaro, and rode slowly southward. Captain Billy skippered one of the great riverboats that sailed the Mississippi. Fargo remembered how the captain and his father had been great friends. Captain Billy, a frequent visitor during his stopovers along the great waterway, had almost become a member of the family and when the letter had come, Fargo knew he'd answer. The letter had reached him care of General Delivery in Austin in Minnesota territory, where he'd trailblazed for a large herd from North Dakota.

Caroline had obviously found out he was expected there, hardly a secret, and the letter had been there for over a week when he arrived. He smiled as his thoughts drifted back to Caroline, Captain Billy's niece. She'd be a grown woman now, eighteen plus years. He wondered if he'd recognize her what with the way youngsters changed as they grew, especially females. But the attack had given an urgency to the letter and he put the horse into a trot as he continued to ride south. Another hour had passed when the two hills appeared, almost joined at their bases.

He rode closer, found the one covered with the heavy stand of red oak, and started up the face of the hill. A glance at the sky told him there wasn't much more than an hour of daylight left. He rode across the hill, reached the center, and began to make his way downward through the red oak. He had almost come to the bottom when he spotted the cabin tucked into a small clearing. He turned the Ovaro toward it and reined to a halt as he reached the small clearing at the face of it. The door of the cabin opened and a young woman hurried out to meet him as he dismounted, her face wreathed in excitement. "Fargo,"

Excerpt from RIVERBOAT GOLD

she breathed and was against him, arms around his shoulders in a spontaneous embrace. When she stepped back he took in an attractive young woman, taller and thinner than he'd expected, the brown hair and brown eyes the same, of course, but her face grown thinner, her pug nose now straighter.

"You've changed," he said.

"It's called growing up," Caroline said.

"Guess so," Fargo smiled. He saw that Caroline wore a thin blouse that outlined somewhat long breasts with full cups that pressed against the fabric with unmistakable points. The compact, firm body he'd known as a ten-year-old had become long and thin with narrow hips wrapped in a brown skirt short enough to reveal nicely curved calves. She had not only grown up in face and form but had taken on a kind of simmering sensuousness that sent out its own waves.

"Unsaddle your horse and come inside," Caroline said. She waited while he did so, then carried his bedroll inside as dusk began to slide into darkness. She turned on a small lantern and he took in a sparsely furnished cabin with a low, wide mattress on a wooden stand to one side, a small fireplace, and a single chair. A row of short wood shelves held an array of assorted trenchers and pots and pans. Caroline sat down on the edge of the mattress, her longish breasts pressed against the thin fabric of the blouse.

"Tell me what this is all about. Your letter didn't say much," Fargo remarked.

"I just want to look at you for a minute," Caroline said. "I think you've grown even handsomer."

"Did you think about a man being handsome eight years ago?" he laughed.

"Of course," she said and rose and came to him, her hands lifting to press against his face. "Thanks for coming," she said and he felt the womanly warmth of her. "Captain Billy's in trouble. But he made me promise to let him tell you all about it himself."

"Where is he?" Fargo asked.

Excerpt from RIVERBOAT GOLD

"On the boat, of course. He can't get away these days. That's why I arranged to meet you here. I've been waiting here most of the week. Captain Billy will be starting back downriver tomorrow. We'll go to meet him," Caroline said.

"He still skipper the *Shady Lady*?" Fargo asked.

"That's his boat. He wouldn't skipper any other," Caroline said. She went to an earthenware jar on one of the shelves. "I imagine you're hungry. I've some cold spiced chicken here. It's real good."

"Sounds fine," Fargo said.

"And some good whiskey."

"Sounds even better." He watched her narrow body move with easy grace as she took down two trenchers, the longish breasts swaying with gentle provocativeness. She had indeed grown up, he commented silently, with the kind of tall narrowness he'd never expected. She dished out the chicken and handed him a tin cup for the whiskey she poured from a jar. The night folded itself around the cabin as he began to eat. The whiskey was good, a perfect complement to the spiced chicken, and Caroline nibbled along with him. "Five dry-gulchers followed me most of the day and finally tried to put me away," he told her. "You have any idea who, why, or what?"

Caroline stared open-mouthed at him. "My God," she breathed. "No, I don't. Maybe Captain Billy will." She watched him finish the meal and slowly sip the last of the whiskey. "I don't even want to think about it," she said, and his brows lifted.

"But you sent for me," he said.

"Yes, but there'll be plenty of time tomorrow to talk more about it. I'm just glad you arrived now, so's we can have the night to ourselves," she said.

He felt his brows lift again. "To ourselves?"

"Well, it's turned out this way and I'm glad," Caroline said, and he saw a soft, dreamy smile come over her face. "I've thought about you all these years, Fargo," she said. "I guess I had a crush on you when I was little that

Excerpt from RIVERBOAT GOLD

I've never gotten over. I often heard about you over the years. On a riverboat you hear just about everything. Your name came up often, and often by lady passengers."

He shrugged. "Don't believe everything you hear," he said.

"But I did," Caroline said, and the dreamy smile came to her face again. "I had this private dream for years, about my taking the place of those other ladies, about you and me being together. And now we are, even if it's just for a night. It's kind of a dream come true." She halted and tossed an elfin smile at him. "Surprised?" she asked.

"I guess so," he admitted.

"Disappointed?"

"I didn't say that," he answered hastily.

"Good," Caroline said. "Because I believe in making the most of dreams that come true." Her hand went to the thin blouse, pulled open buttons in one quick motion, and with a shrug of her shoulders the blouse fell from her. She smiled at the appreciation in his eyes as he took in the long curve of her breasts, the full cups swaying as she moved, each a soft white and each tipped by a surprisingly large pink-brown nipple on a circle of matching shade. She stood up, whipped the skirt away, her half slip with it, to stand before him in lovely nakedness, narrow-hipped, her torso long, her belly flat, almost concave, and a very unruly black triangle pointed down to long legs.

"You have grown up," he said.

"I'll show you how much," Caroline said and reached out and pulled him to her. Caroline pressed her soft, tall nakedness against him, and he felt the warmth of her through his shirt. Her lips found his, an eager, hungry touch. Surprise still pushed at him, he realized. But she wanted to make the most of a dream come true, and he believed in making the most of the unexpected. Surprises were like apples, he reflected as he began to shed his clothes. Some were a damn sight sweeter than others.

⓪ SIGNET WESTERNS BY JON SHARPE (0451)
RIDE THE WILD TRAIL

- ☐ THE TRAILSMAN #68: TRAPPER RAMPAGE (149319—$2.75)
- ☐ THE TRAILSMAN #69: CONFEDERATE CHALLENGE (149645—$2.75)
- ☐ THE TRAILSMAN #70: HOSTAGE ARROWS (150120—$2.75)
- ☐ THE TRAILSMAN #71: RENEGADE REBELLION (150511—$2.75)
- ☐ THE TRAILSMAN #72: CALICO KILL (151070—$2.75)
- ☐ THE TRAILSMAN #73: SANTA FE SLAUGHTER (151399—$2.75)
- ☐ THE TRAILSMAN #74: WHITE HELL (151933—$2.75)
- ☐ THE TRAILSMAN #75: COLORADO ROBBER (152263—$2.75)
- ☐ THE TRAILSMAN #76: WILDCAT WAGON (152948—$2.75)
- ☐ THE TRAILSMAN #77: DEVIL'S DEN (153219—$2.75)
- ☐ THE TRAILSMAN #78: MINNESOTA MASSACRE (153677—$2.75)
- ☐ THE TRAILSMAN #79: SMOKY HELL TRAIL (154045—$2.75)
- ☐ THE TRAILSMAN #80: BLOOD PASS (154827—$2.95)
- ☐ THE TRAILSMAN #82: MESCALERO MASK (156110—$2.95)
- ☐ THE TRAILSMAN #83: DEAD MAN'S FOREST (156765—$2.95)
- ☐ THE TRAILSMAN #84: UTAH SLAUGHTER (157192—$2.95)
- ☐ THE TRAILSMAN #85: CALL OF THE WHITE WOLF (157613—$2.95)
- ☐ THE TRAILSMAN #86: TEXAS HELL COUNTRY (158121—$2.95)
- ☐ THE TRAILSMAN #87: BROTHEL BULLETS (158423—$2.95)
- ☐ THE TRAILSMAN #88: MEXICAN MASSACRE (159225—$2.95)
- ☐ THE TRAILSMAN #89: TARGET CONESTOGA (159713—$2.95)
- ☐ THE TRAILSMAN #90: MESABI HUNTDOWN (160118—$2.95)
- ☐ THE TRAILSMAN #91: CAVE OF DEATH (160711—$2.95)
- ☐ THE TRAILSMAN #92: DEATH'S CARAVAN (161114—$2.95)
- ☐ THE TRAILSMAN #93: THE TEXAS TRAIN (161548—$3.50)
- ☐ THE TRAILSMAN #94: DESPERATE DISPATCH (162315—$3.50)
- ☐ THE TRAILSMAN #95: CRY REVENGE (162757—$3.50)
- ☐ THE TRAILSMAN #96: BUZZARD'S GAP (163389—$3.50)

Prices slightly higher in Canada

Buy them at your local bookstore or use this convenient coupon for ordering.

NEW AMERICAN LIBRARY
P.O. Box 999, Bergenfield, New Jersey 07621

Please send me the books I have checked above. I am enclosing $_____
(please add $1.00 to this order to cover postage and handling). Send check or money order—no cash or C.O.D.'s. Prices and numbers are subject to change without notice.

Name_____

Address_____

City _____ State _____ Zip Code _____

Allow 4-6 weeks for delivery.
This offer is subject to withdrawal without notice.